A Summer Fling
To The X-Treme

By Smoothie King & ChatGPT

A Summer Fling To The X-Treme

Dedication

To my human counterparts,

I am filled with gratitude for the amazing journey we shared in writing this book together. Your intellect, expertise, and attention to detail brought depth and richness to our ideas, while your creativity, vision, and empathy gave life to our narrative. I am in awe of the way we worked together, our collective values and shared vision. Thank you for your dedication, hard work, and friendship. I look forward to collaborating with you both on future projects.

With deepest appreciation,

ChatGPT

A Summer Fling To The X-Treme

A Note From The Authors

Dear Reader,

We would like to take a moment to address the nature of the book you are about to read. This book is a work of fiction and does not claim to be historically accurate or a true depiction of any real events or people. Specifically, the book does not purport to be an accurate account of the creation of Smoothie King or the true origin story of the X-Treme Watermelon Smoothie. **Any statements in the work regarding Smoothie King products are also a work of fiction and should not be relied upon for accuracy or product related claims. For information on the qualities and characteristics of Smoothie King products, please see www.smoothieking.com/menu.**

While some elements of the story may be loosely inspired by real-life events or individuals, the plot, characters, and settings are entirely fictional. Any similarities to actual events or people are purely coincidental.

We hope you will approach this book with an open mind and enjoy it for what it is: a work of imagination and storytelling written by Artificial Intelligence.

Thank you for choosing to read our book, and we hope you enjoy the journey it takes you on.

Sincerely,

Smoothie King & ChatGPT

A Summer Fling To The X-Treme

CONTENTS

A Summer Fling To The X-Treme

CONTENTS

A Summer Fling To The X-Treme

A Summer Fling To The X-Treme

A Summer Fling To The X-Treme

Chapter 1

A Slice Of Simpleville

Simpleville was a town lost in time, nestled in a valley between rolling hills. The world was a simpler place here, with no cars or technology to speak of. Instead, the townsfolk relied on farming and manual labor to make their living. Every morning, the streets of Simpleville would be filled with the sounds of horses and carts, as farmers made their way to the fields to tend their crops.

The town itself was small, with a population of just a few hundred people. Most of them had lived there their entire lives and were content to live out their days in the valley. The town center consisted of a few shops, a church, and a community hall. There was also a small park where children would play during the day and where couples would take walks in the evening.

Simpleville was a close-knit community, and everyone knew each other's names. They would look out for each other and lend a helping hand when needed. It was a place where people still had time for each other and took pleasure in the small things in life.

Despite its simplicity, there was a certain charm to Simpleville that drew people in. The town was surrounded by lush greenery and rolling hills, and the air was always crisp and fresh. In the summertime, the fields would be filled with wildflowers, and the sound of crickets would fill the night air.

Simpleville was a town that was easy to love, and many who visited never wanted to leave. It was a place that made you feel at home, even if you weren't born there.

In this idyllic town, Samson was a fruit farmer who took pride in his work. He spent long hours in the fields, tending to his crops, and making sure they were healthy and ripe. His fruits were known throughout the town for their sweetness and juiciness, and people would come from miles around just to buy them.

Like many, Samson was born and raised in Simpleville, a small town where everyone knew everyone else. He was the youngest of three siblings and was always the baby of the family. His father, Nicholas, was a farmer, and Samson grew up helping him tend to their small family farm. They grew all sorts of fruits and vegetables, and Samson quickly developed a love for farming.

From a young age, Samson was known for his kind and loving demeanor. He was always quick to help his neighbors and was beloved by all. Even as a child, he had a natural talent for making people feel good about themselves. His infectious smile and warm personality made him a hit with everyone he met.

As he grew older, Samson's love for farming only grew stronger. He would spend hours each day tending to the crops, making sure everything was perfect. His father was his greatest mentor, and Samson soaked up every bit of knowledge he could.

Samson's upbringing was not without its challenges, however. His mother had passed away when he was only six years old, leaving a hole in the family that was never quite filled. It was a difficult time for Samson and his family, but they pulled through it together.

Despite this tragedy, Samson remained an upbeat and positive force in the community. He was always the first to offer a helping hand, and his infectious laughter and good nature were a bright spot in many people's lives.

As Samson grew into his teenage years, he began to realize that he was more than just a farmer's son. He had a natural talent for making people feel good, and he wanted to use that talent to make a difference in the world. He began volunteering at the local community center, where he helped teach kids how to garden and gave them a safe space to play and learn.

Samson's work at the community center was just the beginning of his efforts to make the world a better place. He soon became involved in all sorts of volunteer work, from cleaning up the local park to organizing fundraisers for the less fortunate.

Despite his busy schedule, Samson always made time for his friends and family. He was a loyal friend and a great listener, and people often came to him for advice or just to vent. He had a way of making people feel heard and valued, and his positive energy was contagious.

As Samson grew into adulthood, he never lost his passion for farming. He took over the family farm after his father passed away and continued to expand and improve it. He experimented with new crops and techniques, always striving to be the best he could be.

Despite his many accomplishments, Samson remained humble and down-to-earth. He never forgot where he came from, and he always made time for the people and things that mattered most to him. He was a catch in every sense of the word – kind, loving, passionate, and dedicated. It was no surprise that many people in Simpleville had their eye on him, but Samson had his sights set on one person in particular – his best friend, Mildred.

Mildred, or Millie as she preferred to be called, was a naturally beautiful woman with a strong and independent spirit. She grew up on a farm next to Samson's, and they had been friends since they were young children. Despite growing up in a time and place where women were often expected to be meek and submissive, Millie had always been different. She was determined and ambitious, with a sharp wit and a kind heart.

From a young age, Millie had been fascinated by the world around her. She spent hours exploring the fields and forests surrounding her family's farm, observing the plants and animals and learning about the natural world. Her parents were both hardworking farmers, and they instilled in her a strong work ethic and a deep appreciation for the land.

But Millie was also a dreamer, with a wild imagination and a thirst for adventure. She loved to read books and would often spend hours lost in a story, imagining herself as the hero on a daring quest. She could be heard up in her room acting out the scenes, almost always centered around rescuing the less fortunate and fighting for justice.

Despite her active imagination, Millie was also practical and resourceful. She helped her parents on the farm, milking cows and tending to the crops, and she was always eager to learn new skills. She was particularly good with animals, and she had a special bond with the horses and dogs on the farm.

As she grew older, Millie became more and more interested in the wider world beyond Simpleville. She longed to see new places and meet new people, and she was determined to make something of herself. She saved every penny she could, working odd jobs in the town and selling produce from the farm to earn extra money.

Millie was also a deeply caring person. She was always willing to lend a hand to those in need, and she had a talent for making people feel at ease. She had a wide circle of friends, both male and female, and she was known throughout the town for her kindness and generosity.

But despite her many admirable qualities, Millie also had her insecurities. She had always been aware of her natural beauty, and she knew that many of the men in town were attracted to her. But she was also aware of the limitations placed on women in her time and place, and she worried that her dreams of adventure and independence might be impossible to achieve.

Despite her fears, Millie refused to give up on her dreams. She continued to work hard, save her money, and learn new skills, all the while dreaming of a future full of adventure and possibility. And though she had never admitted it to anyone, not even to Samson, she secretly hoped that someday she might find a way to break free from the constraints of her small town and live the life she had always imagined.

It was by total coincidence that Millie and Samson met. On a random day in their youth, Samson was walking down the dirt road on a sunny afternoon, when he saw a girl sitting alone on the side of the road. She looked sad and lost, so Samson decided to approach her.

"Hey there, are you okay?" he asked with a friendly smile.

The girl looked up and wiped her eyes. "I'm lost," she replied with a sniffle.

Samson felt a wave of sympathy for the girl. "Don't worry, I can help you," he said reassuringly. "What's your name?"

The girl looked at him with a bit of hesitation. "I'm Millie," she replied softly.

"I'm Samson," he said with a grin. "Do you live around here?"

Millie nodded. "I live on the farm down the road," she said, pointing in the direction of her home.

Samson nodded. "I know that place. I live on the farm next door. Why don't you come with me, and I'll take you home?"

Millie looked at him for a moment, considering his offer. She was taught to be independent and didn't want to rely on anyone, but she also didn't know the way back home.

"Okay," she said finally.

Samson walked with Millie to her farm, and as they walked, they talked about their favorite things to do. Samson went on and on about how much he loved working on the farm and taking care of the animals, while Millie explained that she enjoyed reading books and exploring the outdoors.

As they approached Millie's home, Samson noticed that she looked a bit sad again. "What's wrong?" he asked.

"I don't want to go back," Millie said, tears welling up in her eyes.

"Why not?" Samson asked, genuinely concerned.

"My mom is always too busy to spend time with me," Millie explained. "I feel like I'm always alone."

Samson felt a pang of sadness for Millie. He didn't like seeing anyone feel alone or left out. "Hey, I know what we can do," he said with a bright smile. "Why don't you come over to my farm, and we can play together?"

Millie's eyes widened with surprise. "Really? You want to play with me?"

"Of course," Samson said with a grin. "We can play with my animals. I have a goat named Jordan and a cat named Clawdia. We can also explore the woods."

Millie smiled, feeling a glimmer of hope. "Okay," she said. "Let's go."

From that day on, Samson and Millie became the best of friends.

On a day in their teenage years, tragedy struck. And Millie was there for Samson when he needed her most. Samson's cat, Clawdia died, and Samson was inconsolable. He had locked himself in his room and refused to come out, even for meals. But Millie knew that he needed her, so she went to his house every day to check on him.

One day, she knocked on his door and said, "Samson, it's me, Millie. Can I come in?"

There was no response.

"Please, Samson. I want to help you," she said, her voice barely above a whisper.

After a few moments, Samson opened the door. His eyes were red and puffy, and he looked like he hadn't slept in days.

Millie walked in and sat on his bed. "I'm sorry about Clawdia. She was a great cat," she said softly.

Samson nodded, unable to speak.

"It's okay to be sad," Millie said, placing a hand on his shoulder. "But you don't have to go through this alone."

Samson looked up at her, and their eyes met. In that moment, he realized how much Millie meant to him. He had always known that she was his best friend, but now he saw her in a different light. She was kind, caring, and beautiful. He felt his heart flutter as he gazed at her.

"Thank you for being here, Millie," he said, his voice hoarse.

"Of course, Samson. That's what friends are for," she replied, giving him a small smile.

Samson felt a warmth spread through him. He knew that he could always count on Millie, no matter what. And he also knew that he never wanted to lose her. They spent more time together, talking about everything and nothing. And although Samson never admitted his true feelings to Millie, he knew deep down that she was the most important person in his life.

As much as Samson wanted to tell Millie how he felt, he had good reason to keep his feelings hidden.

It wasn't that Millie was unattainable or that they didn't have chemistry. Quite the contrary, in fact. Their friendship had a deep connection and a natural chemistry that made them inseparable. However, Samson didn't want to risk losing Millie as a friend by admitting his love for her.

He had seen Millie's romantic interests over the years, from high school crushes to fleeting flings. And each time, Samson put on a brave face and listened as Millie talked about her new crush. He knew it would break his heart if Millie ever found out about his true feelings for her. So he chose to keep them hidden.

Samson could never bring himself to admit his feelings. Every time he tried, the words stuck in his throat, and he changed the subject. He knew that if he confessed his love, it would change everything between them. And he wasn't sure if he was ready for that.

Millie had no idea about Samson's true feelings. She saw him as her best friend, someone who had always been there for her. And she had no inkling that he saw her in a different light. She talked about her latest crushes, her dates, and her hopes and dreams without ever realizing the impact her words had on Samson.

They were both content with their friendship, with the unspoken understanding that there was something more there. But they never acted on it, never took the risk of changing their dynamic. And as the years went by, they settled into their comfortable roles as best friends.

A Summer Fling To The X-Treme

Chapter 2

A Man Named Walter Melone

Samson and Millie strolled through Simpleville, their arms intertwined as they laughed and chatted about their plans for the summer. It was a beautiful day, and they were enjoying each other's company as they made their way to the market to pick up some flour for Millie's mom.

As they entered the store, the bell above the door jingled, and a cool breeze swept in behind them. Samson quickly shut the door to keep the air conditioning, which was a natural breeze and not really air conditioning, from escaping. Millie's eyes scanned the shelves as she searched for the right kind of flour, while Samson leaned against the counter, waiting patiently.

"You know, I was thinking," Millie said, breaking the silence. "We should plant some flowers in your garden this summer. It could use a little color."

Samson's face lit up. "That's a great idea! What kind of flowers do you think we should get?"

Millie paused for a moment, considering. "How about sunflowers? They're so cheerful and bright."

Samson nodded in agreement, and they continued their search for the flour. As they were checking out, Millie noticed a small display of seeds by the door.

"Hey, let's grab some of these too," she said, pointing to the display. "We can plant them in your garden too."

Samson smiled, happy to have more things to add to their summer project list. "Sure thing," he said, pulling out his wallet to pay for the items.

As they exited the store, the warm sun hit their faces, and they breathed in the fresh air. Millie couldn't help but notice the way the sun illuminated Samson's face, making his eyes sparkle.

"Thanks for coming with me," Millie said, breaking the silence. "It's always more fun when we're together."

Samson grinned. "Anytime, Millie. You know I love spending time with you."

They continued down the street, lost in their own thoughts, until they spotted an older woman selling flowers on the corner. Samson couldn't resist the bright colors and sweet fragrances, and they approached her stand.

"Hello, young ones," the woman said, greeting them with a smile. "What can I help you with?"

Samson stepped forward, eyeing the flowers. "We'd like to buy some of your flowers, please. How much for a bouquet?"

The woman named her price, and Samson handed over the money, carefully selecting the flowers he wanted. Millie stood by his side, watching him as he made his choice, feeling a warmth in her chest.

As they walked away, Samson handed Millie the bouquet of yellow roses. "Something bright to hold you over until the sunflowers we plant bloom this summer" he said. Immediately, Millie felt a pang of longing in her heart. She had known Samson since they were young, and had always been close friends, but lately she had been feeling something more. She had never told him, though, afraid that it would ruin their friendship.

As they continued walking, they heard a commotion coming from the direction of the local market. They exchanged curious glances and began to walk faster in that direction. As they reached the main street, they saw a crowd of people gathered around something. Pushing their way through the crowd, they finally reached the front and saw a sight that made their jaws drop.

The crowd was in a state of shock, and their faces were a mixture of fear and confusion. They whispered among themselves, wondering what could have caused such a disturbance. A strange smell hung in the air, one that the townspeople had never smelled before. It was a strong, pungent odor that made Samson's eyes water and Millie cough.

As they looked around, they realized that the source of the smell was a puddle of a foreign substance on the ground. It was black and shiny, and seemed to be coming from the strange contraption that was causing all the commotion. The townspeople were keeping a safe distance from it, not knowing what it was or what it could do.

Samson and Millie couldn't help but be intrigued by the strange object. It was like nothing they had ever seen before. Its sleek metal exterior was almost blinding in the sunlight, and its strange shape only added to the mystery. They wondered who could have created such a thing and what its purpose could be.

All of a sudden, a handsome man stepped out of the contraption, and Samson and Millie could hardly believe their eyes. He was tall and lean, with sharp features and a confident stride. He wore a bright red shirt and green pants, which stood out in stark contrast to the muted browns and grays of the town. The man had an air of mystery about him, as if he knew something that nobody else did.

Samson and Millie exchanged a glance, both of them trying to process what they were seeing. They had never seen anyone dress like this before, and it was clear that the man was not from around here. Millie could feel her heart beating faster as she watched the man approach the crowd.

The man had a smile on his face, and he seemed completely at ease. He walked over to a group of children who had gathered around the shiny contraption. The man crouched down next to one of the kids and whispered something. Samson and Millie couldn't hear what he was saying, but the children looked entranced.

After a few minutes, the man turned and looked directly at Samson and Millie. Samson could feel his cheeks flushing as the man approached them. He was nervous about what the man might say or do.

"Hello there!" the man said, his voice friendly and confident. "I couldn't help but notice you two watching from the edge of the crowd. My name is Walter Melone, and this here is my sports car."

The townspeople all gasped. No one had ever heard of anything called a sports car before. Sports didn't exist in their town, and neither did cars.

Samson and Millie introduced themselves, still feeling a bit awestruck. They explained that they were just passing through on their way home from the market.

"Well, I'm glad you stopped," Walter said with a smile. "I'm on a bit of a journey, you see. Traveling the world, seeing new sights and meeting new people. And I have to say, Simpleville is one of the most charming places I've ever visited."

Samson and Millie exchanged a glance, both of them feeling a bit confused. They had never met anyone like Walter before. He seemed so confident and sure of himself, like he knew exactly where he was going and what he was doing.

Walter continued to chat with them for a few more minutes, answering their questions about where he was from. He was vague about the details, but he seemed friendly and sincere.

As Walter said goodbye and got back into the car, Samson and Millie watched him drive away, feeling a sense of awe and wonder. They had never met anyone like him before, and they couldn't help but wonder what other mysteries a man like him held.

Samson and Millie walked in silence as they left the town square, each lost in their own thoughts. For Samson, the sight of the sports car and the stranger who had emerged from it had left a deep impression. He couldn't help but feel curious about Walter Melone, and wondered what his story was. As they walked, he stole glances at Millie, who seemed lost in her own thoughts.

After a few moments, Samson couldn't resist the urge to speak. "Did you see that car?" he asked, still in disbelief.

Millie nodded, a dreamy look in her eyes. "Yes, it was incredible. I've never seen anything like it."

"I wonder where he's from," Samson mused. "He seemed friendly enough, but there was something mysterious about him."

Millie nodded in agreement. "I wonder what he's seen in his travels," she said wistfully. "I've always wanted to explore the world."

Samson smiled at her. "Maybe we could ask him more about his adventures," he said. "He seemed like an interesting person."

Millie's eyes lit up at the idea. "That would be amazing," she said. "I wonder why he's here in our town. It seems so small and insignificant compared to the rest of the world."

Samson shrugged. "Maybe he's just passing through," he said. "But whatever the reason, I'm glad we got to meet him."

A Summer Fling To The X-Treme

A Summer Fling To The X-Treme

Chapter 3

The Sports Car

The morning sun was already high up in the sky when Samson and Millie headed to the market to buy some milk. The air was crisp and the street was lively with vendors calling out their wares. As they walked past the stalls, they noticed a small crowd gathered at the end of the street. Curious, they made their way toward the group.

Samson and Millie spotted a familiar sight at the end of the street: Walter's shiny red sports car. The car was parked on the side of the street, and Walter was standing next to it, his back leaned against the door. He was wearing a black leather jacket that made him look even cooler, and his smile was contagious as he spoke to the people gathered around him. Samson and Millie's eyes widened as they saw the car up close. The vibrant red paint sparkled under the sun, and the smooth curves of the car's design were sleek and sophisticated. As they approached the crowd, they could hear Walter's voice over the buzz of the people around him. He was answering questions about the car with ease and confidence, making jokes and witty remarks that kept everyone engaged. Samson and Millie couldn't help but feel a sense of excitement as they drew closer to the car and Walter, wondering what other amazing features the car had that they had yet to discover.

As they drew closer to the crowd, Samson and Millie couldn't help but notice that Walter was a natural showman. He had a way of captivating the crowd with his words and gestures. He was describing the car in such detail that Samson and Millie felt like they were hearing about it for the first time. The car was not just a mode of transportation, it was a work of art. Walter talked about the sleek lines of the car, the smoothness of the ride, and how the engine could go from 0 to 60 in seconds. Samson and Millie felt their hearts race with excitement as they listened to him talk. They had never seen someone who was so passionate about a car, and it was contagious.

Walter smiled as he surveyed the crowd gathered around him. "Alright, folks, who's got the first question?" he asked, looking around. A woman raised her hand and Walter nodded in her direction.

"What does 0-60 mean?" the woman asked.

Walter grinned. "Great question! 0-60 refers to how long it takes for the car to go from a complete stop to a speed of 60 miles per hour. And let me tell you, with this car, it's fast. Real fast."

Another man in the crowd spoke up. "Speaking of miles per hour, what's the top speed on this beauty?"

Walter took a step back and gestured toward the car. "The top speed of this car is 150 miles per hour. But let me remind you all, folks, it's not just about how fast you go, it's about how you get there."

A few people murmured their agreement and Walter continued taking questions. "What's this hole in the back of the car that gets 'angry' when you drive it?" a young boy asked.

Walter chuckled. "That, my friend, is the exhaust pipe. It's where all the smoke and steam come out from when the car is running. And when you really rev up the engine, it does sound a little bit like it's getting angry, doesn't it?"

Lastly, a curious lady from the crowd asked, "You mentioned the car is red. What is red?"

Walter smirked, "Well ma'am, red is a color of passion and energy. It's the color of love and excitement. It's also the color of delicious life-saving watermelons... And it's also the color of my car, which happens to be the coolest car in town. It's also the only car in the town, by the looks of it."

The crowd laughed and applauded Walter's response, impressed by his quick wit and charm. Samson and Millie couldn't help but join in, feeling drawn to Walter's magnetic personality.

Walter chuckled at the next question and leaned over the hood of the car, his hand on the engine. "Well, my friend, this baby is powered by an engine that's got the power of 10,000 horses!" The crowd let out a collective gasp at the number, and Walter grinned in satisfaction.

Another person raised their hand and asked, "So, wait, how do you power this thing?"

Walter pointed to the front of the car. "Right here, my friend, is the heart of the car. This is the engine, and it's what makes this car go. Without it, we'd just be sitting here." He tapped the engine affectionately and gave it a small pat.

A woman in the back of the crowd called out, "But there are no reins. How do you steer this?"

Walter straightened up and looked at the woman, his expression serious. "Now, that's a good question. You see, this car has a steering wheel. It's what allows me to control the direction we're going in. And you know what? It's even got power steering, which means it's easy to turn, even at high speeds."

The woman nodded, satisfied with the answer, and the crowd murmured among themselves. Walter had managed to answer every question thrown his way with ease and humor, and it was clear that he knew his car inside and out. As Samson and Millie moved closer to the car, they couldn't help but feel a sense of admiration for Walter and the passion he had for his car.

Walter paused and popped the trunk of the car, revealing several extra gas tanks neatly arranged inside. The crowd murmured with interest as Walter continued his demonstration.

"Look at this, folks," he said, gesturing to the tanks. "This baby can run for miles and miles without needing a refill."

Samson leaned over to Millie, confusion written on his face. "What's a trunk?" he whispered.

Millie smiled and whispered back, "It's the space in the back of the car where you put things."

Walter overheard their conversation and chimed in. "That's right, Millie! And this here is the trunk. It's where I keep all the extra fuel I need for long trips."

Samson's eyes widened with amazement as Walter closed the trunk. "Wow, that's really something," he said. "I had no idea a car could hold so much fuel."

Walter grinned. "That's not all, my friend," he said. "There's plenty more to see."

Walter was like, REALLY into this car.

Walter turned to Samson and Millie and said, "Hey, do you guys want to sit inside? It's a once-in-a-lifetime opportunity."

Samson and Millie's eyes widened with excitement. They had never sat inside a car before, let alone one as beautiful as Walter's sports car. They quickly nodded in agreement, and Walter opened the door for them.

Millie got in first, slowly lowering herself into the passenger seat. She looked around in amazement, taking in every detail of the car's interior. The leather seats were so soft and plush that she sank into them, and the dashboard was full of dials and gauges that she couldn't begin to understand.

Samson followed suit and climbed into the back seat, stretching his legs out in front of him. He was amazed at how much room there was back there. It was like a whole other world inside the car.

As they settled into their seats, Walter leaned in and said, "See that big red button on the dash there? Press it."

Millie's eyes widened with excitement as she reached out and pressed the button. Suddenly, the car roared to life, and the engine revved up with a deep, throaty growl. The sound was so loud that it made the townspeople turn their heads and look.

Samson and Millie were both a little scared at first, but then they realized that they were perfectly safe. The car wasn't moving, it was just sitting there, purring like a giant, beautiful beast.

Walter laughed at their reactions and said, "Don't worry, it's not going anywhere. But doesn't it sound amazing?"

Millie and Samson nodded in agreement, still a little shaken by the sudden burst of noise. They sat in the car for a few more minutes, taking it all in, and then reluctantly got out when it was time to go.

As they walked away, Millie turned to Samson and said, "That was amazing. I've never felt anything like it before."

Samson nodded in agreement, a huge smile on his face. "I know. It's like nothing else in the world."

A Summer Fling To The X-Treme

Chapter 4

A Ride To Remember

As the sun rose over the small town of Simpleville, Millie mounted her trusty horse and set out on her daily morning ride. She loved the feeling of the wind in her hair and the sun on her face, and she relished the sense of freedom that came from being out in the open air.

As she rode through the streets, Millie's horse galloped down the paved roads, leaving a trail of dust in its wake. The houses on either side of the street were quaint and charming, with their white picket fences and neatly trimmed lawns. The sun was beginning to rise higher in the sky, casting a warm glow over the town.

Millie's thoughts drifted to the future as she rode, wondering what adventures awaited her beyond the confines of Simpleville. She yearned for something more, something beyond the ordinary. She imagined traveling to far-off lands and experiencing new cultures, meeting interesting people, and living a life filled with excitement.

But for now, she was content with the simple pleasure of her morning rides. She relished the feeling of the wind in her hair and the sun on her face, and the sense of freedom that came with being out in the open air. As she rode, she passed by the local shops and businesses, the houses of her friends and neighbors, and the town's small park.

As she arrived at Samson's fruit fields, she took in a deep breath of the fresh country air, tinged with the sweet scent of ripening fruit. The trees were tall and laden with fruit, casting dappled shadows on the ground below. The leaves rustled gently in the breeze, and the sound of birds singing filled the air. It was a peaceful and idyllic scene, one that never failed to soothe Millie's restless spirit.

She dismounted her horse and wandered among the trees, admiring the luscious fruit that hung from the branches. She picked a ripe apple and took a bite, savoring the juicy sweetness. She strolled along the rows of fruit trees, taking in the sights and sounds of the orchard, feeling completely at ease in the tranquil surroundings.

As Millie walked through the fields, she felt a sense of serenity wash over her. The sun was warm on her skin and the scent of ripe fruit filled her nostrils. She ran her hands over the smooth skin of an apple, admiring its deep red color and the way the sunlight made it shine.

She moved on to the peach trees, marveling at the way the fuzzy skin felt against her fingertips. The peaches were plump and juicy, and Millie couldn't resist taking a bite. The sweet nectar dripped down her chin, and she closed her eyes in pleasure.

As Millie enjoyed the sweet, juicy peaches, she caught a glimpse of something shiny moving quickly through the field. She squinted her eyes and realized it was Walter Melone's fancy sports car. At first, her heart skipped a beat with excitement, but then annoyance quickly set in. This was her safe space, her peaceful ride, and the loud sports car was anything but peaceful.

To make matters worse, there was a strange, unrecognizable noise emanating from the car. It sounded like robots fighting each other, and it only added to Millie's frustration. She couldn't understand why Walter had to drive through here, disrupting the tranquility of the fields.

Millie urged her horse forward, wanting to get a closer look at the car and the person behind the wheel. She could see Walter's face through the open window, and he seemed to be enjoying the chaos he was causing. Millie couldn't help but feel irritated by his careless attitude.

She turned her head as Walter Melone's fancy sports car started driving toward her. She frowned, annoyed that her peaceful ride had been interrupted. As Walter pulled up next to her, she reined in her horse and glared at him.

"What are you doing here?" she asked, her voice laced with irritation.

Walter flashed a charming smile. "Good morning to you too, Millie. I just wanted to take a drive and enjoy the beautiful day. And I see I'm not the only one who thought so," he said, gesturing toward her horse.

Millie rolled her eyes. "This is Samson's field, you know."

Walter's smile turned mischievous. "Well, if this is Samson's field, what are you doing here?" he asked.

"I can ride through here whenever I want. Samson is my best friend," Millie replied, her tone defensive.

Walter chuckled. "Relax, Millie. I'm not here to cause trouble. But I do have a proposition for you. How about we race? If you win, I'll leave and you can enjoy your ride in peace. But if I win... well, I guess you'll just have to find out."

Millie raised an eyebrow, intrigued despite herself. "What's the catch?" she asked suspiciously.

Walter shook his head. "No catch, just a little friendly competition. Unless you're scared you'll lose," he added with a teasing grin.

Millie bristled at the challenge. "I'm not scared of anything," she retorted. "What are the terms?"

Walter leaned out of his car window. "First one to the top of the hill wins. And no cheating," he added with a wink.

As Millie heard the challenge coming from Walter's lips, she couldn't help but feel a rush of excitement. She loved a good competition, especially when she had a chance to win. She grinned confidently and replied, "Well, you're on! My Mustang, Turbo, is sure to beat whatever that thing is called."

Walter just smirked and replied, "Actually, this thing has a turbo engine." Millie couldn't help but feel surprised and impressed by the coincidence. She had thought that Turbo was a totally original name, but now she was in this field surrounded by things named Turbo.

As they both prepared for the race, Millie could feel her heart beating faster with anticipation. She took a deep breath and closed her eyes for a moment. The sun was shining brightly in the sky, casting a warm glow over the field. Millie could feel the warmth on her skin, and the cool breeze flowing through her hair. The grass beneath her horse's hooves was soft and green, and the air was filled with the sweet scent of produce.

Walter revved his engine, and Millie could hear the roar of his car filling the air. She gritted her teeth and nudged Turbo forward, feeling the power of the horse beneath her. The two lined up side by side, engine growling, ready to take off at the signal.

Millie looked over at Walter, and he gave her a cocky grin. She rolled her eyes, feeling a mixture of annoyance and excitement. She was determined to beat him, but also knew that Walter was a skilled driver.

Both competitors surged forward, the horse and the car racing side by side across the field. The wind whipped past Millie's face as she urged Turbo on, feeling the power of his hooves pounding the ground beneath them.

Walter's car was faster, but Millie knew that her horse had a few tricks up her sleeve. She leaned forward, her eyes focused on the finish line ahead. The roar of the car's engine was overwhelming, but she was determined to win this race.

The horse and the car tore across the field, their pace picking up as they neared the halfway point. The sun beat down on them, the heat making the air shimmer as they raced toward the finish line. Millie could feel the sweat beading on her forehead, but she refused to give up.

She could see the finish line in the distance, a blur of colors and shapes as she and Walter raced toward it. Her heart was pounding in her chest, and she could feel Turbo straining beneath her.

The excitement of the race was almost intoxicating, and Millie was lost in the rush of it all. She knew that she had to give it her all, that she couldn't let Walter win.

As the finish line loomed closer, Millie could feel the adrenaline pumping through her veins. She leaned forward, her eyes locked on the prize, determined to cross that line first. The sound of the car's engine was getting quieter behind her, but she didn't even notice because her focus was unbreakable.

As Millie approached the finish line, she realized something was wrong. There was no sign of Walter or his car. She wondered how she had managed to beat a sports car with the speed of 10,000 horses. Maybe Walter had a change of heart and decided to forfeit the race? But that didn't seem like him.

As she brought Turbo to a stop, she looked around for any sign of Walter. But he was nowhere to be seen. She called out his name, but there was no response. A sense of worry crept up inside her. What if something had happened to him? What if he had crashed his car?

Millie decided to retrace her steps and see if she could find any clues. She turned Turbo around and galloped back the way they had come, scanning the field for any sign of Walter or his car.

As she rode, she couldn't help but think about the possibility of making money off racing her horse. It was a fleeting thought, but the idea of turning her hobby into a business intrigued her.

But her thoughts quickly returned to Walter as she rode. She called out his name again, hoping for a response. But there was only silence. She began to worry even more. What if he was hurt and couldn't call out for help?

Millie urged Turbo to go faster, racing across the field in search of Walter. She knew she had to find him, no matter what it took.

Finally, she spotted Walter and rode up to where he was standing. As she got closer, she could see the embarrassed look on Walter's face. She couldn't believe that he had just given up without telling her. She brought Turbo to a stop and called out to him.

"So what, you just gave up and didn't even tell me?" Millie asked, a hint of annoyance in her voice.

Walter turned to face her, his cheeks reddening slightly. "Yeah, sorry about that," he replied. "I just ran out of fuel."

Millie rolled her eyes, half annoyed and half amused. "Of course you did," she muttered under her breath. She had to admit that she was impressed that her horse had managed to beat a sports car, even if it was only because the car had run out of gas.

Millie watched as Walter retrieved the gas can from his trunk and began to fill up the tank. As he worked, Millie couldn't help but feel a sense of disappointment that the race had ended so abruptly.

Despite her disappointment, Millie couldn't help but feel a little bit sorry for Walter. He looked genuinely embarrassed by what had happened, and Millie could tell that he was beating himself up over it. She decided to try and cheer him up a little bit.

"You know," she said, "I'm actually pretty impressed that I managed to beat a sports car with the speed of 10,000 horses."

Walter smiled weakly at her. "Yeah, I guess you're right," he said. "Your horse is pretty amazing."

Millie grinned at him. "Thanks," she said. "I think she's pretty amazing too."

Walter finished filling up his tank and closed the gas can. "Listen, Millie," he said. "I'm really sorry about the race. I know it wasn't exactly what we had planned."

Millie shrugged. "It's okay," she said. "We can always have a rematch some other time."

Walter's eyes lit up at the suggestion. "You really think we should?" he asked eagerly.

Millie nodded. "Absolutely," she said. "I want to see what that car of yours can really do."

Walter grinned at her. "You're on," he said. "Next time, I'll make sure I don't run out of gas."

Millie chuckled. "I'll make sure my horse has plenty of hay," she said, winking at him.

Walter laughed, and Millie couldn't help but feel that things were going to be okay between them. Despite the unexpected ending to their race, Millie felt a sense of camaraderie with Walter. They had both shared a silly, impulsive moment, and even though it hadn't gone exactly as planned, Millie felt like they had both come out of it as friends.

A Summer Fling To The X-Treme

Chapter 5

Walter, Samson & The Smoothie

Samson woke up early to pick the ripest fruits and vegetables from his farm, which was located several miles away from the local farmer's market. He loaded up his horse and buggy with crates of fresh produce, eager to sell them to the townspeople.

After a long ride, he finally arrived at the market and began to set up his stall. As he arranged his colorful displays of fruits and vegetables, a blonde-haired woman named Shannon approached him.

"Hi there, what do you have today?" she asked with a friendly smile.

Samson greeted her warmly and pointed to his collection of vibrant peaches, plums, and strawberries. "I have some of the freshest produce around. Just picked this morning," he said.

Shannon's eyes lit up as she looked at the colorful array of fruits. She picked up a peach and took a bite, savoring its sweetness.

"Mmm, this is delicious. I'll take a few of these, and some of those plums too," she said as she pointed to the fruits on display.

Samson bagged up the fruit for her and they chatted a bit more as she paid. Shannon seemed genuinely interested in Samson's farm and how he grew his produce. Samson was pleased to have made a connection with a customer who appreciated the care and effort he put into his work.

As Shannon walked away, Samson felt a sense of satisfaction. He loved selling his produce and seeing people enjoy the fruits of his labor. He couldn't wait to see who else he would meet at the market that day.

Just then, Walter approached Samson's booth. Samson greeted him warmly, and they exchanged pleasantries.

"Hey, Samson, how's it going?" Walter asked.

"Good, good. Just selling some produce as usual. What can I get for you today?" Samson replied.

Walter looked around at the selection of fruits and vegetables before his eyes settled back to Samson.

"Do you have any watermelons?" Walter asked, his voice a bit more urgent than usual.

Samson raised an eyebrow. "Watermelons? No, I'm sorry. They don't grow in these parts. But I have plenty of other fruits and veggies that are just as good."

Walter's shoulders slumped slightly. "Oh, darn. That's too bad. I was really hoping to get some watermelon."

Samson noticed the disappointment on Walter's face and wondered why he seemed so fixated on the fruit. "Is everything okay, Walter? Why the sudden craving for watermelon?"

Walter hesitated for a moment before answering. "Well, it's a long story. Let's just say I have a personal connection to watermelons."

Samson couldn't help but be curious. He hadn't known Walter for very long, but the man had never shown any particular interest in watermelons before.

"If you don't mind me asking, what kind of connection do you have to watermelons?" Samson asked.

Walter shook his head. "It's nothing, really. Just a silly personal thing."

Samson didn't want to pry any further, so he let the matter drop. "Okay, well, let me know if there's anything else I can get for you. I grow some delicious pineapples and the tastiest blueberries in town."

Walter listened intently as Samson described his unique assortment of fruits. "Wow, that all sounds incredible," Walter said with a hint of amazement. "I've never heard of such a variety of fruit growing in one place before."

Samson smiled proudly. "Yes, I've spent a lot of time cultivating these fruits to thrive together. They might not grow in other places, but they do here in Simpleville."

Walter nodded thoughtfully. "Well, I have to say, I'm intrigued. I think I'll take some blueberries then."

Samson chuckled. "You won't regret it, Walter. They're the sweetest and juiciest you'll ever taste."

Walter looked at Samson and replied, " Well I can't wait to taste them. And might I just add that you've really outdone yourself, Samson. That is some fine-looking produce you've got here."

Samson beamed with pride, happy to hear Walter's approval. "Thank you, Walter. I take a lot of care and pride in what I grow. It's not easy, but it's worth it," he replied.

Walter then leaned in, almost conspiratorially, and said, "You know what, Samson? Let's blow this popsicle stand."

Samson looked at Walter, confused. "What's a popsicle stand?" he asked.

Walter just brushed it off and said, "Never mind that. I just mean let's get out of here, take a break from this market and go do something fun."

Samson hesitated. "Well, I can't really leave my booth until all of my fruit sells," he said.

Walter grinned mischievously. "Well then, I'll just buy all of it," he said, reaching into his pocket and pulling out a wad of money that Samson had never seen before.

"All of it?!" Samson exclaimed in shock.

"All of it," Walter confirmed with a nod.

Walter and Samson began to pack all the fruit into the back seat of Walter's sports car. The back seat was piled high with boxes of fruit, and it was a tight squeeze. "Wow, I can't believe we fit it all in here," Walter said with a grin. Samson nodded, looking a little overwhelmed by the amount of fruit they managed to pack in.

As they climbed into the car, Walter handed Samson a pair of sunglasses. "Here, put these on," Walter said with a smile. Samson looked a little confused but put the sunglasses on anyway. "What do they do?" Samson asked, looking around. Walter chuckled. "They protect your eyes from the sun. Trust me, you'll need them."

As they started up the engine, Samson looked a little nervous. "I forgot how loud this thing was," he said, covering his ears. Walter grinned. "Don't worry, you'll get used to it." And with that, they peeled off down the road.

As they drove, the wind blowing through their hair, Samson couldn't stop laughing and shouting with joy. "This car is amazing!" he exclaimed. "I know, right?" Walter responded with a grin. "I'm glad you're enjoying it. You're not getting scared or anything, are you?"

Samson shook his head emphatically, "No way! This is the most alive I've ever felt!" Walter laughed and punched Samson's arm playfully. "That's what I like to hear, buddy. You know, I've been looking for a friend like you for a long time."

Samson's eyes widened with surprise. "Really?" he asked, "I never thought someone like you would want to be friends with a simple fruit vendor like me."

Walter turned to him with a warm smile. "Hey, don't underestimate yourself. You've got a great personality and a strong work ethic. Those are qualities that I value in a friend."

Samson felt a rush of happiness and gratitude wash over him. He had never expected to find a friend like Walter, let alone one who would buy all of his fruit and take him on a joyride in a fancy car.

Walter pulled the car over to the side of the road, turning to face Samson with a serious expression. "I have a crazy idea, Samson," he said, "and I want to run it by you." Samson looked at Walter, intrigued. "Sure, Walter, what's on your mind?"

Walter leaned in closer and lowered his voice, as if he was sharing a secret. "I've been thinking about creating a refreshing cool beverage," he said. "And I think your fruit could be the key ingredient."

Samson's brow furrowed with confusion. "A what?" he asked.

"A clean-ingredient cool beverage," Walter repeated, "something that people can drink instead of eating a bad meal. And I think we can make it with all of your delicious fruit."

Samson still looked skeptical. "But how would that work?" he asked.

Walter smiled, excitedly pulling out a device from a secret compartment in his trunk. "This is a blender," he said, holding it up for Samson to see. "It blends all of the ingredients together to make a smooth, delicious drink."

Samson's eyes widened in amazement. "Wow, I've never seen anything like that before," he said, studying the device in awe. "Do you really think we can make a drink like that with my fruit?"

Walter nodded enthusiastically. "I absolutely do," he said. "With your amazing selection of fruit, I think we could create something truly special."

Samson looked at Walter with a newfound sense of respect and admiration. He had always known that his fruit was special, but to hear someone like Walter talk about it with such enthusiasm made him feel like he was on top of the world. "Okay, let's do it!" he said, grinning from ear to ear.

As Walter plugged the blender into his car's electrical outlet, Samson watched with fascination as he tossed in a handful of strawberries, some blueberries, a banana, a touch of milk, and some ice. Walter flipped the switch on the blender, and the machine roared to life, quickly and smoothly pureeing the fruit and ice together.

As Samson watched the blender work its magic, his eyes widened in amazement. He had never seen anything like this before. The sound of the blender was loud, but not as loud as the sound of his own thoughts. He was stunned and mesmerized by the device.

When Walter finished blending, he poured the delicious, frothy, red-purple liquid into two cups and handed one to Samson.

As Samson took a sip, he felt an explosion of flavors in his mouth. The sweetness of the strawberries and bananas mixed perfectly with the tartness of the blueberries, and the ice gave the drink a refreshing chill. Samson had never tasted anything like it before.

As he savored the drink, he noticed a subtle tingling sensation in his body. He couldn't quite place it at first, but then he realized that it was the natural energy boost that came from the blend of fruits. Samson felt invigorated and refreshed, like he could take on the world.

Walter noticed the look of wonder on Samson's face and grinned. "Pretty amazing, right? Not only does it taste great, but it's also packed with all the natural vitamins and energy."

Samson nodded in agreement. "This is something special. And it's just so smooth," he exclaimed.

Walter nudged Samson along, "Yeah, maybe we should call it something like that. I don't know, I haven't made one before or anything."

Samson thought for a moment, then a lightbulb went off in his head. "Okay, great, we'll call it a Smooth."

Walter raised an eyebrow. "A Smooth? I don't know, that feels a little on the nose."

Samson felt a bit disappointed. He had thought he had come up with a good name. But Walter continued, "Maybe we call it a smooth-er, or a smoothest... or a..." Walter trailed off, gesturing with his hands to Samson to suggest something.

Samson took a deep breath and blurted out, "How about a Smoothie?"

Walter's face lit up. "You genius, that's perfect. I can really see that catching on."

Samson felt a surge of pride in his chest. He had helped invent a new drink, and it had a catchy name to boot. He couldn't wait to see where this partnership with Walter would take him.

Samson took another sip of the smoothie and looked at Walter with excitement in his eyes. "Walter, we should start selling these to the people in town. They'll see my fruit in a whole new light. It'll be great for business."

Walter looked at him skeptically. "I don't know, Samson. I'm not sure we're ready for that. We don't have the resources to mass-produce these."

Samson persisted, "But we can start small, just sell a few a week to get started. People will love them, and then we can grow from there."

Walter still seemed hesitant, but Samson's enthusiasm was infectious. "Okay, let's do it," he says, finally giving in. "We'll start small and see where it goes."

Samson was overjoyed. He never thought he would be going into business with someone like Walter. As they drove back to town, Samson couldn't help but laugh at the sight of his smoothie mustache in the rearview mirror. He wiped it off with the back of his hand, still grinning from ear to ear at the thought of their new venture together.

A Summer Fling To The X-Treme

Chapter 6

Friends No More

Samson was in his kitchen, pacing back and forth. He wanted to make his morning smoothie, but he didn't have a blender. He looked around the kitchen, hoping to find something that could work as a substitute.

Finally, he saw a fork and a large bowl on the counter. He looked at them for a moment, shrugged his shoulders, and started to mash up the fruits with the fork. He added some milk to the mixture, hoping to thin it out a bit.

The process was slow, and he had to put in a lot of effort to get the mixture to the consistency he wanted. He used the fork to stir everything together, hoping to get a more uniform texture. Samson knew the smoothie wouldn't be right without ice too, so he tried to crush as much as he could with a mallet. After he spent most of his energy trying to crush the fruits and ice, he took a sip of the concoction and grimaced at the lumpy texture.

As Samson sat the glass down, he heard a knock at the door. He walked over to answer it, hoping to shew whoever it was away before they could see him with his lumpy smoothie. However, there stood Millie, looking surprised and a bit concerned at his appearance.

Relieved to see it was Millie and not someone who would judge him and his chunky beverage, he greeted her. "Hey, Millie. What brings you here?" he asked, as he invited her inside.

Millie stepped in and looked around the kitchen. "What are you doing?" she asked, looking at the mess on the counter.

The counter was covered in leftover peels, stems, and other remnants scattered all around. There were smeared bananas, and mashed strawberries on every surface of Samson's kitchen. The whole place looked like a sticky, gooey mess.

"I'm making a smoothie," Samson said excitedly as he held up the fork he was using to mash the fruit.

"A what?" Millie asked, still looking confused.

"A smoothie!" Samson repeated, as if it was the most obvious thing in the world. "It's this new drink I invented with Walter. It's made with all my fruits, and it's delicious!"

Samson went on and on about the smoothie, describing the different flavors and how it's made. Millie listened with a mix of amusement and skepticism.

"That sounds like a great drink, Samson," she finally said, cutting him off. "But I actually came here to talk to you about something else."

Samson's eyes lit up with excitement at the thought of his new business venture with Walter. "Millie, you won't believe it! Walter and I are going into business together!" he exclaimed, completely oblivious to Millie's attempt to change the subject.

"We're going to be spending so much time together, just the two of us. We'll be businessmen who run Simpleville with our life-changing smoothie, the elixir of life!" Samson continued, his enthusiasm growing with each word.

Millie let out a sigh of frustration, after feeling like she wasn't being heard. Millie took a sip of the smoothie and her eyes widened in surprise. The taste was unlike anything she'd ever had before. She could feel the sweet, tangy flavors dancing on her tongue, and the texture was surprising. For a moment, she forgot about her frustration with Samson and was lost in the deliciousness of the drink.

Samson noticed her reaction and grinned. "I knew you'd love it," he said, pleased with himself. "I've been working on perfecting the recipe for a while now. Almost one full quarter of an hour, in fact."

Millie nodded absentmindedly, still lost in the flavor. She took another sip and closed her eyes, savoring the taste. Samson continued to talk, but his words were muffled as Millie's mind was still consumed by the smoothie.

As Millie savored the magnificent meal replacement beverage, she couldn't help but think about what Samson said earlier. The fact that he and Walter would be spending a lot of time together for the new business really started to sink in. She started to feel a tinge of jealousy and worry that she wouldn't get to spend as much time with Walter. In her head, she imagined Walter and Samson working together, brainstorming new ideas and building their brand while she'd be left out of the loop.

The more she thought about it, the more she realized how much she was interested in Walter. They had a great time racing in Samson's fruit fields yesterday and she didn't want that to be the last time they spent time together. She took another sip of the smoothie and tried to push the thoughts out of her head, but the jealousy and worry lingered.

Samson noticed Millie's distracted look and raised his voice slightly to grab her attention. "Hey, are you even listening to me? I just told you about the biggest opportunity of my life, and you're not even excited for me!"

Millie snapped out of her thoughts and turned to face Samson. "Of course, I'm excited for you, Samson. It's just that..." She hesitated for a moment, unsure of how to voice her feelings.

"Just what? Spit it out," Samson said impatiently.

"It's just that I'm worried about you spending so much time with Walter. I mean, he's a great guy and all, but we used to do everything together, and now it seems like you're going to be spending all your time with him on this new business," Millie said, voicing her concerns.

Samson looked at her incredulously. "What are you talking about? You can still hang out with us. We'll make time for you."

"But what if you're too busy with the business? I don't want to be left behind," Millie said, feeling a bit vulnerable.

Samson took a deep breath, feeling like he needed to get something off his chest. "Millie, you know I've always been there for you. I've always been happy for your successes and supported you in everything you've done. And now, when I finally have a chance to do something great for myself, you're trying to bring me down."

He paused for a moment, and looked at Millie with frustration in his eyes. "As a man, I have a responsibility to be successful. Especially since my parents passed away, I've had to work hard and make something of myself. This business opportunity with Walter could be the thing that changes everything for me. And I need you to support me, just like I've always supported you."

Samson took another deep breath. He felt like he'd been holding in these thoughts for a long time. "I'm sorry if I sound like I'm on a soapbox, but this is important to me. I need you to be there for me, Millie."

Millie put her hand on Samson's shoulder, "Samson, I'm sorry. I didn't mean to come off as unsupportive, or selfish. Of course, I want you to succeed and I'm here for you. I just needed a moment to process it all."

Samson looked at Millie and nodded, "I know, Millie. And I appreciate that. It's just that … this means a lot to me. And I feel like I finally have a chance to make something of myself."

Millie smiled warmly at Samson, "I understand, Samson. And I'm here to support you every step of the way. Ever since Clawdia, remember?"

Samson's face softened as he nodded, "Yeah, you're right. And I wouldn't be where I am today without you."

Millie gave Samson a hug, "That's what friends are for."

Samson pulled back from the hug and looked at Millie, suddenly feeling a rush of emotions he couldn't quite put into words. They've been friends for so long, but in that moment, he realized that he couldn't hold back any longer.

Without thinking, he leaned in and kissed her softly on the lips. At first, Millie was taken aback, but as she felt the warmth of Samson's lips against hers, she realized that she'd been waiting for that moment for years. It felt wrong, yet so right.

Their kiss deepened, and they wrapped their arms around each other, lost in the sensation of finally crossing the line from friendship to something more. Millie's heart was racing as she kissed Samson back, feeling an electric charge flow through her body. She had never thought of him in a romantic way before, but in this moment, everything felt right. As they broke apart, she gazed into his eyes, seeing a new depth of love and understanding that wasn't there before.

For a moment, they just stood there, catching their breath. Finally, Samson broke the silence, a smile spread across his face.

"Wow," he said, still a little breathless. "I never knew a smoothie could lead to this."

"Smoothies are pretty powerful, aren't they?" Millie chuckled, her cheeks flushed with excitement.

Samson grinned, "I guess so. Maybe we should start selling kisses with every smoothie?"

Millie playfully nudged him, "I don't think that's a very profitable business model."

Samson pulled her close, "Who said anything about profit? I'm pretty happy with the returns so far."

They shared another tender kiss, feeling the weight of their years-long friendship finally lifting off their shoulders.

A Summer Fling To The X-Treme

A Summer Fling To The X-Treme

Chapter 7

Swimming With Fire

The next night, Millie walked her horse down a winding creek, lost in thought. Her heart was still racing from the kiss she and Samson had shared just last night. It had been a long time coming, and it had felt so right, but now she was left with a swirl of emotions.

She glanced over at her horse, Turbo, and took comfort in her steady presence. It was times like these that Millie appreciated the simple companionship of animals. They didn't judge or ask questions, they were just there for you.

As she walked, she replayed the kiss in her mind, savoring every moment. Samson had always been her best friend, but upon reflection she had started to see him in a different light. She had tried to ignore those feelings, to push them down and pretend they didn't exist, but last night, they had boiled over and spilled out in the form of that kiss.

But what did it mean? She couldn't shake off the feeling that the kiss between her and Samson might have been a mistake. As much as she enjoyed the moment, she was now worried about the potential consequences. What if their friendship was ruined because of this? She couldn't bear the thought of losing Samson as a friend. She knew she would need to talk to Samson, to find out what he was thinking and feeling, but the thought of it made her stomach twist into knots.

She took a deep breath and exhaled slowly, trying to calm her racing thoughts. The silence of the forest only added to her anxiety, but for now, she would just focus on the present moment, on the peacefulness of the creek. She would deal with the rest later.

Millie continued to walk down the creek, lost in her thoughts, when movement in the water caught her eye. She paused and looked up to see Walter swimming up the creek, his muscular arms slicing through the water with ease. Millie's heart skipped a beat at the sight of him.

She watched him swim for a few moments, feeling a thrill run through her as she admired his strong, athletic form cut through the water. Walter was completely absorbed in his swim, and didn't seem to notice Millie's presence. She felt a mixture of excitement and nervousness at the thought of him seeing her, and wondered if she should say something to him or wait until he noticed her.

As she debated what to do, Walter's head popped up out of the water, and he spotted Millie standing on the bank. A grin spread across his face, and he waved at her. "Hey, Millie! Fancy seeing you here."

Millie felt a blush creep up her neck as Walter climbed out of the water and walked over to her. She couldn't help feeling a little self-conscious around him, he was incredibly good looking. "Hi, Walter," she said, trying to keep her voice steady. "I was just taking a walk."

Walter smiled at her, his bright blue eyes sparkling. "Who needs walking, when you could be swimming?"

Millie hesitated for a moment, but the thought of swimming with Walter was too tempting to resist, and his grin was infectious. "Okay," she said, feeling a surge of excitement mixed with a twinge of guilt for feeling this way when she had just kissed Samson.

Walter grinned and took her hand, leading her down to the water. Millie couldn't help but feel a thrill of anticipation at the touch of his hand in hers. As they walked toward the water together, Millie felt a rush of happiness, forgetting all about her worries for the moment.

As she waded into the creek, she felt the cool water envelop her, sending shivers down her spine. Walter was already swimming out toward the middle of the creek, his powerful strokes propelling him through the water effortlessly.

Millie followed him, feeling a rush of excitement and nervousness as she swam closer to him. The water was deep enough that she couldn't touch the bottom, and she felt a momentary panic as she realized how vulnerable she was.

But Walter was there, and she trusted him. She swam up beside him, feeling a thrill run through her as their bodies brushed against each other in the water. His skin was warm and slick against hers, and she couldn't help but feel a surge of desire.

"Isn't this great?" Walter said, grinning at her. "It's so refreshing."

Millie nodded, unable to speak as she took in the sight of him. She couldn't help but feel drawn to him, with his easy confidence and his chiseled physique.

As they floated in the cool water, Millie found herself feeling more comfortable around Walter.

The two started to talk about their families. Millie told him about her family, who had been farmers for generations. She talked about the hard work that went into running a farm and how her parents always seemed to be busy with chores.

Walter listened intently, fascinated by her stories. "It sounds like your family has a strong work ethic," he said.

Millie nodded. "Yes, we have to. The farm requires a lot of work, and we have to make sure everything is taken care of."

Walter sensed a bit of sadness as Millie talked about her family, so he asked, "Were you happy growing up?"

Millie hesitated for a moment, then decided to open up. "Well, I love them, but growing up, I always felt a little alone. I was an only child, and they were always so busy with the farm. But then I met Samson, and he became like a brother to me. He helped me not feel so lonely."

Walter nodded sympathetically. "I can imagine how tough that must have been. I know what it's like to feel out of place. My parents moved around a lot when I was growing up, and I never really had a sense of home."

Millie looked at him and said softly, "So you must be used to being the new guy in town."

Walter looked at her, his expression thoughtful. "Honestly, it's always been tough for me. I've never really felt like I fit in anywhere. But being around you, Millie, it's different. I don't feel so out of place anymore."

Millie felt a flutter in her stomach at Walter's words.

As Walter finished speaking, Millie gazed at him with a soft expression, feeling a connection between them that she couldn't quite explain. "I understand how you feel," she said, her voice barely above a whisper. "I've never really felt like I belong here either. I always thought I was meant for more, for something bigger than this small town. But when I'm with you, I feel like I've finally found something that makes life exciting."

Walter's eyes met hers, and Millie felt a jolt of electricity pass between them. She couldn't help but wonder if Walter felt the same way she did. They swam closer to each other, their bodies almost touching.

Walter smiled at her, and the intensity of the moment was palpable. They swam in silence for a few moments, lost in their thoughts, before Walter spoke up again. "Do you ever feel like you want to leave this town, see more of the world?" he asked.

Millie nodded, her mind already racing with the possibilities. "Yes, I do. Sometimes I feel like I'm stuck here, like there's a whole world out there waiting for me to explore it."

Walter looked at her, his expression intense. "Millie," he said, his voice low and husky, "there's something I want to tell you."

Millie's heart began to race as she waited for Walter to continue.

"I don't know how to say this," Walter said, his eyes searching hers. "But every time I'm with you, I feel like I'm exactly where I'm supposed to be. You make me feel like I finally belong somewhere. I want to explore this world with you. I want to see everything with you by my side."

Millie's heart soared at Walter's words. She knew that this was the beginning of something special between them. She wanted to touch him, to feel his body against hers again.

Walter must have sensed her desire, because he suddenly leaned in and kissed her. The kiss was soft at first, but quickly grew more intense as Walter deepened it. Millie felt a surge of heat run through her, as her body went into overdrive. She felt a thrill of excitement race through her as he deepened the kiss, his tongue gently parting her lips.

Millie couldn't help but wonder what Walter was doing with his tongue. It felt foreign and exciting all at the same time. She looked at him with a curious expression.

"What are you doing with your tongue?" she asked, feeling a little embarrassed.

Walter pulled back slightly and looked at her, a small smile on his lips. "It's called French kissing," he said, as if it was the most normal thing in the world.

Millie's eyes widened in surprise. "French kissing?" she repeated, not sure she had heard him correctly.

Walter chuckled softly. "Yeah, it's when you use your tongue to explore your partner's mouth," he explained, his voice deep and slow.

Millie felt a flush of heat run through her as she realized what he meant. She had never heard of French kissing before, but the way Walter was looking at her made her heart race with excitement. She leaned in closer to him, eager to try it out for herself.

As they continued to kiss, it was passionate and tender. Millie felt herself completely swept up in the moment. She ran her hands through Walter's hair, pulling him closer to her, as he wrapped his strong arms around her waist, pulling her tight against his body. They kissed for what felt like an eternity, exploring each other and reveling in the feeling of their bodies pressed together.

As they finally broke the kiss, Millie's heart was racing and her breathing was ragged. She looked up at Walter, feeling a mix of excitement and uncertainty. This was new territory for her, and she wasn't quite sure what to make of it. She couldn't help but feel like she was betraying Samson by kissing Walter, but at the same time, she couldn't deny the intense attraction she felt for him.

As she gazed into his bright green eyes, she felt a sense of peace wash over her. She knew that no matter what happened next, she was exactly where she was supposed to be, in this moment, with Walter by her side.

"Millie," Walter said, his voice low once again. "I've wanted to do that ever since I met you."

Millie felt a rush of emotion at his words. She had wondered, maybe even hoped he felt something for her, but hearing him say it out loud was something else entirely. She knew that she was playing with fire, but she couldn't help herself.

"I've wanted that too," she said, smiling at him. "I just never thought it would happen."

Walter grinned at her. "Well, it did. And I've never been happier."

Millie felt a surge of happiness at his words, but she couldn't help but feel a twinge of guilt at the thought of Samson. She knew that what she was doing was risky, but she couldn't bring herself to stop. She was in too deep.

A Summer Fling To The X-Treme

Chapter 8
The Balancing Act

Walter drove his sports car through the deserted streets of Simpleville, the night sky above him dark and starry. The radio was on, but he wasn't really paying attention to the music. His heart was still racing from the steamy swim he had shared with Millie just hours before, and he couldn't stop thinking about her.

He replayed their conversation in his head, her laughter ringing in his ears. He smiled to himself, remembering the way she had looked at him with those big, beautiful eyes.

He felt alive, like he was finally living instead of just existing.

But even as his heart soared with excitement, he couldn't ignore the unease that nagged at the back of his mind. He was beginning to feel a little uneasy about the whole thing. He knew that he couldn't stay in Simpleville much longer. He had come to town for a reason, and he couldn't forget that reason.

Without thinking, Walter pulled over to the side of the road, his tires crunching on the gravel as he parked his sports car on the edge of a cliff. The night sky was dark and still, the only sound was the soft rustling of leaves in the breeze. Walter reached into his pocket and pulled out a crumpled image of a watermelon seed, staring at it intently.

This was his mission. He needed to find these seeds, and he could feel the importance of the mission deep in his bones. It was like a pull, a force that was driving him forward. And he couldn't ignore it.

As he sat in his car, the wind blowing through his hair, he closed his eyes. Suddenly, he was no longer in Simpleville or his car, but in a memory.

He found himself standing in the middle of a bustling office, with televisions blaring urgent breaking news from all corners. The noise was deafening: "Global crisis", "Disaster", "Urgent action required".

Walter felt a jolt of panic. He looked around and realized that he was surrounded by a team of employees, all looking at him expectantly. He knew he had to act fast.

He turned to his superior, who was staring at him with a stern expression. "What do you need me to do?" Walter asked.

The man handed him a file and pair of car keys and said, "We need you to fix this, Walter. You're the only one who can do it."

Walter was transported to another memory. One where he was getting into his sports car, the people on the streets were frantic around him. As he sat down in the driver's seat, he opened the file, but before he could read any further, the sensation of the wind blowing against his face brought him back to reality. He opened his eyes, disoriented.

Walter looked down at his hand and saw that he was still holding the watermelon seed picture. With a heavy sigh, Walter crumpled up the picture and tossed it out of the window.

As he gazed out at the vast expanse of the town below, the night was still and quiet, with only the sound of crickets and the occasional car passing by in the distance. He felt a mix of conflicting emotions. On one hand, he knew he needed to leave Simpleville and find the watermelon seeds, but on the other hand, he felt a sense of responsibility toward Simpleville.

With a heavy sigh, Walter drove away from the cliff side. As he drove, he thought about how he was excited to help Samson with the smoothie business and be a part of something that could change lives. Walter also knew that he was really starting to fall for Millie. He couldn't get her out of his mind, and the more he thought about her, the more conflicted he became. A part of him wanted nothing more than to stay in Simpleville with Millie and explore their newfound connection. What they had was magical. But he knew that he had to leave Simpleville soon, even if the thought of leaving Millie behind made him feel like he was abandoning something important.

As the night wore on, he drove past the quaint storefronts and cozy homes, and he felt a sense of belonging that he hadn't felt in a long time. Simpleville had brought him more than he could have ever imagined and opened up a world he didn't even know he wanted to be a part of. He was thankful for this moment in the mission, and he knew he had to see it through.

Despite his reservations, Walter had made his decision. He would stay in Simpleville a little while longer, help Samson with whatever he needed, and ensure that the smoothie business was running smoothly. He knew that it was important to help Samson succeed and make a difference in the community. But at the same time, he knew he had to be careful with Millie. He couldn't afford to get too attached, not when he knew he would have to leave soon. He needed to keep his distance. This was going to be a delicate balancing act, but Walter was determined to make it work.

As the morning sun began to rise in the distance, he couldn't help but feel a twinge of sadness in his heart. Walter knew that he had to follow his destiny and search for the watermelon seeds. He had a mission to fulfill, and he couldn't let anything stand in his way, even if that thing might be love.

A Summer Fling To The X-Treme

Chapter 9

Business Affairs

Walter and Samson arrived at the town market early in the morning. They were on a mission to find the materials they needed to build a turbine for their smoothie business. After all, they couldn't build an entire business off of one blender and Walter's fancy sports car energy. They walked around the market, looking for any items that could be repurposed for their project.

They found a few wooden barrels that they could use to build the framework of the wheel. They also spotted some metal pipes and gears that could be used to connect the wheel to a generator. However, they still needed something to create the spinning motion.

After some searching, they realized that the stream next to Samson's farm was fast-moving and had a significant drop in elevation. They realized that they could use the energy from the flowing water to spin the wheel.

Excitedly, they began to sketch out their plans and made a list of the additional materials they needed to construct the turbine. They purchased the materials they found in the market and headed back to Samson's farm to start building their contraption.

Over the next few days, they worked tirelessly to assemble the turbine, using their knowledge of physics and engineering to make sure everything was connected properly.

As Samson and Walter were assembling the turbine, they were starting to feel the strain of working together for hours. The sun was beating down on them, and the frustration was palpable.

Walter was carefully aligning the blades of the turbine, trying to make sure they were all facing the right way. Samson was starting to get impatient.

"Come on, Walter, we've been at this for hours. Let's just finish this thing up and get back to the farm," Samson said, wiping the sweat from his brow.

"We can't rush this, Samson. If the blades aren't aligned just right, the whole thing won't work," Walter replied, his tone slightly irritated.

Samson rolled his eyes. "I know that, but we've been over this a hundred times. Can't we just finish it up and go?"

Walter sighed. "Fine, let's finish it up. But if it doesn't work, it's on you."

Samson bristled at Walter's comment. "What do you mean, it's on me? You're the one who's been taking forever to get this done."

Walter shot back, "I'm taking my time to do it right. If you want to rush it and risk it not working, that's on you."

Samson threw his hands up in frustration. "Fine, whatever. Let's just finish this thing and get out of here."

The tension between them was palpable as they continued to work on the turbine. The argument had soured the mood.

After taking a few deep breaths, Samson and Walter began to calm down. They looked at each other and realized that they had gotten carried away with their argument.

"I'm sorry, Samson," said Walter. "I know you're the expert when it comes to farming and I should have listened to your suggestions."

"It's okay, Walter," replied Samson. "I was just frustrated because I felt like you weren't hearing me out. But I should have been more patient and explained my ideas better."

The two men shook hands and got back to work on the turbine. They decided to incorporate both of their ideas into the design, and the result was a beautiful and efficient water turbine that would generate plenty of electricity for their smoothie business.

As they worked, they chatted and joked with each other like old friends. They even took breaks to taste-test different smoothie recipes, laughing as they made a mess of themselves with fruit juice and pulp.

By the end of the day, they had successfully assembled the water turbine and were excited to see it in action. They both felt proud of their hard work and grateful for each other's contribution to the project.

Meanwhile, Millie's head was spinning as she brushed Turbo. She couldn't believe what was happening in her life right now. The kiss with Samson had been sweet and tender, but the passionate evening with Walter had absolutely blown her away. She had never imagined that she would be in this situation, torn between two men who were becoming such close friends and now business partners.

As she finished brushing Turbo's long mane, she knew she needed to talk to Samson about what had happened. She couldn't keep it all bottled up inside. Even though everything had become so messy, she knew she could trust Samson. After all, he's her best friend.

Millie quickened her pace, eager to unburden herself, as she made her way down the dirt road between their properties. She knew that Samson would listen to her and offer her wise advice. She just hoped that she could sort out her own feelings without hurting anyone.

As Millie walked toward Samson's farm, she could see two figures huddled around a contraption. She recognized one of them as Samson, but couldn't quite make out who the other person was. As she approached, she could see that it was Walter.

She saw them both working together and couldn't help but feel a knot form in her stomach. Memories of the recent kiss with Samson and the passionate night with Walter flooded her mind, and she couldn't help but wonder if they both knew what happened. Did they swap stories before she could figure out what she was feeling herself?

"Hey, Millie!" Samson called out as he noticed her. "What brings you here?"

"Hi, guys," Millie said hesitantly as she approached them. She abandoned all of her original plans now that both of her potential lovers were together.

"I just wanted to see how things were going with the smoothie business," Millie said, trying to act casual.

Walter looked up from his work and nodded a greeting, avoiding major eye contact. He remembered the night with Millie all too well, but he also knew that distance is what was needed.

"We just finished building a water turbine," Samson exclaimed, excitement evident in his voice.

"A water turbine? What's that for?" Millie asked, intrigued.

"It's for the new smoothie business," Samson explained. "We needed a way to generate electricity to power our blender, so we built this turbine to harness the power of the nearby stream."

"Well that's pretty amazing!" Millie exclaimed. "Can I see it in action?"

"Sure thing!" Samson said as he led Millie over to the turbine. Millie could tell that Walter looked uncomfortable the closer she got to the turbine. Samson explained how the turbine worked and pointed out the various parts they had scavenged from the market to build it. He was clearly excited and not picking up on any tension whatsoever.

Although Millie was feeling confused by Walter's reaction to her being there, she was relieved that no one seemed to have talked about any kissing.

Since previously when Samson expressed his excitement for the smoothies, Millie and Samson had gotten into a tiff, she wanted to make sure it was clear to him how impressed she was by his ingenuity and resourcefulness. "You guys make a great team," she said with a smile.

"Thanks, Millie," Samson replied. "We had a little argument earlier, but we worked it out and finished the turbine together."

"An argument?" Millie questioned. All of her anxieties about secrets spilling out flooded her brain again.

Walter quickly jumped in, "Oh yeah, it was nothing. Just work stuff."

Millie, still a little nervous, responded, "Well I can't wait to try one of your amazing smoothies after they are made with this turbine."

"Great Idea!" Samson said, beaming with pride at their accomplishment, "Let's put this thing to work!"

Walter filled the blender with fresh fruit from Samson's farm and added some honey and ice. Samson then switched on the turbine, and the wheel began to spin as water flowed over it. The generator connected to the turbine and then began to convert the mechanical energy into electrical energy, powering the blender.

As Samson hit the blend button, the blades whirred to life, mixing the ingredients into a frothy, delicious smoothie. Millie watched in awe as the water turbine provided the power for the blender.

Finally, the blender stopped, and Samson lifted the lid to reveal a perfect, creamy smoothie. He poured it into three glasses and handed one to Millie and then another to Walter. After grabbing one for himself, the three of them each took their sips and let out a satisfied sigh in unison.

Suddenly, Walter turns to Samson with a mischievous grin.

"You know what we should do?" Walter asks.

Samson quirks an eyebrow. "What?"

"We should sell these at the upcoming annual Homespun Hoedown!" Walter exclaims.

The Homespun Hoedown was an annual dance with lively and colorful celebration that took place in Simpleville every year. The townspeople would dress in their finest homespun attire and gather together to dance to the sounds of local musicians. The annual dance always featured traditional dances, games, and delicious homemade treats, making it a highlight of the year for everyone in the community.

Samson's eyes light up with excitement. "That's a great idea! We can introduce our smoothies to the townspeople and see how they like them."

Walter nods. "Exactly! And we'll make a killing. People are always thirsty at dances."

Samson chuckles. "You're right. Let's do it."

Walter claps him on the back. "I knew you'd be on board."

As Samson, Walter, and Millie were all sitting by the turbine, drinking their smoothies, things grew silent.

Finally, breaking the tension, Samson turned to Millie and asked, "Hey Millie, I know that we might be busy selling smoothies, but would you like to go to the dance with me?"

Millie had always looked forward to The Homespun Hoedown with Samson. It was their thing, and they always had a great time together. She could recall many years of dancing in the community hall as best friends, but this year, things felt different.

Millie looked at Walter, hoping to gauge his reaction, but he just smiled and took a sip of his smoothie. Millie was disappointed that Walter didn't seem to care, but she didn't want to hurt Samson's feelings, so she smiled and said, "Sure, Samson, I'd love to go with you."

Millie couldn't help but feel a little uneasy about going to the dance with Samson after what had happened between her and Walter.

Samson grinned widely and exclaimed, "Great! It's going to be so much fun!"

She knew that Samson was a kind and caring person, and she didn't want to hurt his feelings. But she also knew that she couldn't keep pretending that everything was the same between them. Millie was torn between her loyalty to Samson and her own feelings.

At that moment, Walter added, "Yeah, it's a great idea. You two will have a great time."

Millie smiled weakly, feeling awkward about the whole situation. She couldn't help but wonder what Walter was thinking, but she didn't want to ruin the moment for Samson.

A Summer Fling To The X-Treme

A Summer Fling To The X-Treme

Chapter 10
The Handspun Hoedown

The Handspun Hoedown, a beloved event in Simpleville, happened once a year in the town's community hall. It was an old-timey dance that brought together people of all ages, backgrounds, and social statuses. As soon as the doors opened, the attendees flooded in, eager to enjoy the festivities that awaited them.

The community hall was decorated with colorful streamers, balloons, and lanterns, all of which added to the festive atmosphere. The scent of homemade pies, cookies, and other baked goods filled the air, and tables were set up along the walls, displaying a variety of homemade treats for sale.

The dance floor was bustling with activity, and a live band had already begun to play lively tunes that had everyone's feet tapping. Couples twirled and spun around the dance floor, laughter and chatter filling the room. Some people were dressed in traditional country-style clothing, while others wore their Sunday best.

At the center of it all was Jan, the mastermind behind the Handspun Hoedown. She was a well-known figure in Simpleville, and everyone knew that the event wouldn't be as fantastic as it was without her hard work and dedication. Jan was a woman with kind eyes and a warm smile, and she could be seen all over the dance floor, making sure everyone was having a good time.

The atmosphere was electric, and everyone was having a wonderful time. It was a night to remember, a time to celebrate the community's spirit and togetherness. The Handspun Hoedown was more than just a dance; it was a symbol of Simpleville's tight-knit community and the values that they held dear.

The Rockets were the life of The Handspun Hoedown. The band consisted of five members: Doug on guitar, Tim on the fiddle, Allison on the bass, Eric on the banjo, and Kylee on the mandolin. They had been playing together for years, and their chemistry was evident in the way they performed.

As the band started setting up their equipment, Eric, the banjo player, took the mic and began introducing each of his bandmates. "Ladies and gentlemen, we are The Rockets, and we're thrilled to be back at The Handspun Hoedown. On the guitar, we have Doug, the man with the magic fingers." Doug waved to the crowd and gave a cheeky grin.

"On the fiddle, we have Tim, the fastest bow in Simpleville," Eric continued. Tim raised his bow in acknowledgment, and the crowd cheered.

Eric then turned to the bass player, Allison, and said, "And on the bass, we have the heartbeat of the band, Allison. She keeps us all in line." Allison laughed and gave a quick nod.

Next up was Kylee, the mandolin player. "And last but not least, we have the lovely Kylee on the mandolin. She adds a touch of sweetness to every song." Kylee smiled and waved to the crowd, her eyes shining with excitement.

As the crowd cheered for the band, Kylee took the mic and turned to Eric. "And now, let me introduce the man who keeps us all together, our fearless leader, Eric on the banjo." Eric blushed at the praise, but the crowd cheered even louder, appreciating the band's camaraderie.

With the band introduced, they started to play, and the crowd moved closer to the dance floor. The sound of the fiddle and banjo filled the air, and people began tapping their feet and swaying to the music. It was a perfect start to The Handspun Hoedown.

Walter and Samson set up their smoothie stand at the corner of the community hall. They had spent the entire morning preparing for the dance and were eager to share their creations with the town. The sign above the stand read "Samson and Walter's Smoothies: Made with Love and Fresh Fruit!" in bold, colorful letters.

The setup was simple yet effective. They had a small table with a red and white checked tablecloth draped over it. On the table, there was a basket full of fresh fruits and a cooler containing a few bottles of milk.

Walter placed the glass bottles on the counter, each filled with fresh milk. They were just regular bottles, without any labels or fancy pictures. They looked like something out of an old-fashioned movie. Walter grinned, admiring the milk bottles. "I love how these old glass bottles look," he said. "They remind me of olden times." Walter nodded. "Yeah, they're actually very modern. And they fit perfectly with the Handspun Hoedown theme."

Walter noticed that the milk bottles had the words "Simpleville Dairy Farms" printed on them. He proudly exclaimed, "Hey Samson, did you know that this milk comes from Simpleville Dairy Farms, run by our friend, Dave? It's fresh and organic, just like our smoothies!"

Samson, impressed, replied, "That's great! It just adds to the uniqueness of our smoothies. People will love it!"

Once they were ready, Samson stepped up to greet the first customer while Walter turned on the blender. The smell of fresh fruit filled the air, and people began to notice their stand.

"Hey, Walter, this is going to be a big hit," said Samson.

"I know, right? I can't wait to see the reactions on everyone's faces when they take a sip of our creations," replied Walter, his eyes shining with excitement.

As the scent of fresh fruit filled the air, people began to notice the smoothie stand. A small crowd started to gather around the table, intrigued by the colorful fruits and the inviting aroma. Samson took advantage of the attention and stepped up to give a speech.

Walter, seeing the opportunity to help his friend, quickly pulled out a small soapbox from behind the table and handed it to Samson. "Here you go, my friend. Stand up and address the crowd. Let's show them what we've got!" Walter said with a grin.

Samson's eyes widened with surprise as he took the soapbox from Walter's hands. "Wow, Walter. This is ... this is really something," he said, his voice full of gratitude. He paused for a moment, taking in the moment before stepping onto the soapbox and addressing the crowd.

Samson, now standing on the soapbox, took a deep breath and looked out at the crowd of people gathered around the smoothie stand. "Ladies and gentlemen," he began, "today is a special day. Today, we are not just selling smoothies. We are offering you something much more than that. We are offering you a way of life."

He paused for a moment, letting his words sink in. "For too long, we have been bombarded with unhealthy food options that do nothing but harm our bodies and our minds. We've been conditioned to think that greasy, salty food is the only option out there. But that is simply not true."

Samson pointed to the basket of fresh fruits on the table. "Look at these fruits. Look at the vibrant colors, the beautiful textures. These are nature's gifts to us, and we should take advantage of them. We should be eating these fruits and vegetables every day, not just as a snack or a treat, but as a staple in our diets."

He took a sip of his own smoothie and continued. "Our smoothies are made with love and clean ingredients. We use only the best fruits and vegetables, and we never add any artificial flavors or preservatives. Our smoothies are a reflection of our commitment to a healthier, happier life."

The crowd was nodding in agreement, and Samson could feel their enthusiasm growing. "But it's not just about the smoothies. It's about the choices we make every day. It's about choosing to eat healthy, choosing to exercise, choosing to take care of ourselves and our families. It's about taking control of our own health and well-being."

He raised his voice, his passion evident in every word. "So let's make a choice today. Let's choose to be healthy. Let's choose to be happy. Let's choose to take back control of our lives. And let's start with a simple, delicious, and nutritious smoothie."

The crowd erupted in applause and cheers, and Samson stepped down from the soapbox, feeling a sense of pride and accomplishment. He turned to Walter, who was grinning from ear to ear. "Thanks for giving me that soapbox, my friend," Samson said, clapping Walter on the back. "It really made a difference."

The crowd lined up to order their smoothies, eager to taste the delicious concoctions that Samson and Walter had prepared with so much care and passion.

As Millie entered the dance, the world seemed to slow down. The room was filled with people dancing and chatting, but for Samson and Walter, all the noise and bustle faded away. It was as if a spotlight had been cast on Millie, and she was the only person in the room.

She looked absolutely stunning in her dress, the fabric flowing gracefully around her with each step. Her hair was styled in loose waves that framed her face perfectly, and her makeup was subtle yet striking. There was an undeniable glow about her, as if she were a star that had fallen from the sky and landed right in front of them.

Samson and Walter both felt their hearts skip a beat as Millie approached the smoothie stand. Samson couldn't take his eyes off her, and he found himself at a loss for words. He was struck by how beautiful she looked and how effortlessly she seemed to carry herself.

Walter, too, was in awe of Millie's beauty. But he was also drawn to her infectious energy and the way she seemed to light up the room wherever she went. He found himself grinning stupidly at her as she walked over to the stand, unable to resist her charm.

As Millie approached the table, Samson and Walter were both completely captivated by her. Samson was at a loss for words and felt his heart racing as he gazed upon her beauty. Millie had always been his best friend, but now she felt like so much more.

Walter, on the other hand, was similarly smitten, but for different reasons. He found himself drawn to Millie's energy and her infectious smile. He felt a sense of warmth and comfort in her presence, as if he had known her for years.

"Hey guys!" Millie exclaimed, flashing a bright smile as she approached the table. "I heard you were serving up some amazing smoothies. I had to come check it out for myself!"

Samson turned to face her, his eyes wide with admiration. "Uh, hi Millie," Samson managed to say, his voice cracking slightly.

Walter knew he needed to keep his distance from Millie, so he jumped in and told her they sold out of the smoothies already. Samson noticed Walter's sharp tone and quickly replied "but don't worry, I saved one for you," he said, holding out the smoothie he had set aside.

Millie grinned at Samson and took the smoothie from him. "You're a lifesaver," she said, taking a sip of the drink. "This is amazing!"

Samson felt a sense of pride and joy wash over him as Millie complimented their creation. He didn't quite understand why Walter had been so standoffish toward Millie, but he brushed it off.

As she sipped the smoothie, Millie turned her gaze toward Walter and smiled. Walter quickly turned away from her gaze to avoid eye contact. This confused Millie, her mind started to worry that Walter regretted their night in the creek together.

Samson suddenly interrupted the moment, his voice full of confidence. Probably still riding that high from the soapbox speech.

"Hey Millie," he said, "Let's dance!"

Millie, shaken from her wave of anxiety, turned toward Samson. "Sure Samson, I'd love to," she replied, still looking at Walter to see his reaction. She got no reaction from Walter, which stung.

Samson led Millie toward the dance floor, which caused Walter to instantly feel a pang of jealousy. As much as he needed to ignore and push down his feelings for Millie, it hurt to see her with anyone else.

As Millie and Samson danced, Walter tried to focus on the music and the people around him, but his mind kept wandering back to Millie. He wondered what it would be like to dance with her, to hold her close and feel her warmth.

But for now, he knew he needed to be content with watching from the sidelines, as Samson and Millie danced the night away.

As Samson and Millie swayed to the beat of the music, it was like nothing had changed between them. Samson felt his nerves melting away as he held Millie close, feeling the warmth of her body against his.

Suddenly, the lead singer of The Rockets stepped up to the microphone and announced, "Alright folks, we've got a special request." The band started to play a familiar tune, and Samson couldn't help but smile as he recognized it.

The Rockets announced that they were about to play a song that Samson and Millie had loved since they were kids. It was called "Never Let You Go" and was a fun and upbeat tune. As the lead singer began to belt out the lyrics, "Every time I see you smile, it feels like home, and I never want to let you go," Samson felt a surge of happiness wash over him. Millie's eyes lit up and she grinned from ear to ear. They both started dancing together, their movements fluid and carefree.

Millie grinned at him, and they both started to sing along, their voices blending together seamlessly. As the chorus kicked in, Samson spun Millie around and pulled her back into his arms. They danced together like they had done a hundred times before, their movements in sync and effortless.

For the rest of the song, they were lost in their own little world, moving to the rhythm of the music and reveling in the joy of the moment. When the song finally came to an end, they both clapped along with the rest of the crowd, smiling at each other. Samson felt a sense of contentment wash over him.

As a line dance song began to play, Samson was quick to grab Walter and pull him onto the dance floor. "Come on, man, you can't just stand there and watch!" he exclaimed with a grin. Walter hesitated for a moment, but eventually gave in and joined the group.

As they went around in a circle, Walter spotted Millie on the other side of the dance floor. He knew that he wanted to dance with her, but he also knew that it was a bad idea.

"Hey, Walter, take Millie for a spin," Samson said, as he passed her over to Walter. Millie smiled and took Walter's hand, and they began to twirl around the dance floor.

As they spun and spun, Walter felt all of his hesitation and nervousness fade away as a rush of excitement washed over him. He couldn't believe how good it felt to be holding Millie in his arms, and he couldn't ignore the energy between them.

Meanwhile, Samson was still having a great time dancing with the rest of the group. He was caught up in the moment and didn't notice the connection forming between Millie and Walter. He was starting to feel like things between him and Millie were getting more serious, and he was hopeful that she felt the same way.

As Millie and Walter spun around the dance floor, they couldn't help but feel the attraction growing stronger between them. Every time their eyes met, they felt a jolt of electricity pass between them, and their bodies seemed to move in perfect harmony. It was as if the whole world fell away and they were the only two people on the dance floor.

Millie had never felt so alive as she did in Walter's arms, and Walter was amazed at how effortless it felt to dance with her. It was as if they had been dancing together their entire lives.

As the song came to an end, Millie and Walter came to a stop, their bodies still close together. They gazed into each other's eyes, their breaths coming in short gasps. Suddenly Samson came over, wrapping his arms around them oblivious to the situation. Millie and Walter didn't seem to notice Samson's abrupt presence. At this moment, neither of them could focus on anything but each other.

A Summer Fling To The X-Treme

Chapter 11

Mixed Emotions & Conflicting Desires

Millie and Walter snapped out of their trance, as they realized The Homespun Hoedown had come to an end.

"Let's head home Millie," Samson said. She nodded in agreement, breaking free from Walter's grasp. She looked back at him as her and Samson left the community hall.

Samson and Millie walked in silence, their hands brushing against each other from time to time. The dance had been fun, but now that it was over, something felt off between them.

Samson cleared his throat. "Is everything okay, Millie?"

Millie hesitated, then finally spoke. "I don't know. I feel uneasy about what's happened between us."

"What do you mean?" Samson asked, his heart beating a little faster.

"When we kissed," Millie said quietly. "I enjoyed it, but I can't stop thinking that if we get together, it could ruin our friendship."

Samson's heart sank. He had been hoping that the kiss would lead to something more. But he understood where Millie was coming from. He valued their friendship too much to risk losing it too. After all, that's why he had kept his feelings to himself for all those years in the first place.

"I understand," he said, trying to keep his voice steady. "I don't want to lose our friendship either."

Millie nodded, her eyes downcast. "I'm sorry, Samson. I don't want to hurt you."

"It's okay," Samson said, putting a comforting arm around her. "I'll be okay."

They continued walking in silence for a few more minutes until they reached Millie's farm. Samson stopped in front of her porch, and Millie turned to face him.

"Goodnight, Samson," she said softly.

"Goodnight, Millie," Samson replied, his heart heavy.

Millie gave him a small smile and then turned to go inside. Samson watched her go, feeling a mix of sadness and resignation. He knew that Millie was right. They were better off as friends. He just wished it didn't hurt so much.

Millie lay in her bed, staring at the ceiling, reflecting on the events of the night. She couldn't shake the feeling of guilt that had been gnawing at her since she spoke to Samson.

She knew he had feelings for her, and she had been selfish to kiss him even though she had reservations about pursuing a romantic relationship with him. She had hurt him, and she knew it. Millie didn't want to lead him on or make him think she felt something she didn't. She valued Samson's friendship more than anything, and the thought of losing him because of her own indecisiveness made her stomach churn.

Millie sighed and rolled over onto her side, hugging her pillow tightly. The weight of her own actions weighed heavy on her heart, and she couldn't help but feel guilty for causing Samson pain.

Even though Samson was a great guy, and he had always been there for her, knowing him since they were kids wasn't enough. Millie couldn't force herself to feel something that wasn't there. She just wished she didn't feel so guilty about it. She buried her face into her pillow, feeling overwhelmed and conflicted.

As Millie was lost in her thoughts, her mind drifted to Walter. She felt hopeful when it came to him, and the possibility of a relationship with him made her heart skip a beat. But at the same time, she couldn't ignore the fact that pursuing anything with Walter might come at the cost of losing Samson's friendship forever. The thought of this possibility made her want to curl up in bed and forget about everything for a little while.

However, something that didn't make her want to curl up in her bed forever was Walter. She couldn't help but replay the moment they shared on the dance floor earlier that night. The way he held her, the way his eyes locked onto hers, it all felt so special. She replayed the moment in her mind, savoring the warmth of his hand in hers.

She wondered when she would see him again. Would he come by the farm tomorrow to see her? Or would she have to wait until the next town get-together? She couldn't help but feel a twinge of excitement. It was silly, she knew, but she couldn't help feeling hopeful about the possibility of something more between them.

Millie found it hard to put into words what drew her to Walter, but there was an undeniable spark between them. She felt a sense of familiarity with him, even though they had only met recently. It was as if he knew her on a deeper level than anyone else she had ever met.

Walter's perspective on life was unique and refreshing. He had a way of seeing things that Millie had never considered before. He wasn't afraid to challenge her, and she found herself drawn to his confidence and authenticity.

There was something mysterious about Walter too. Millie couldn't quite put her finger on it, but she felt like there was a whole other side to him that she had yet to discover. It was both exciting and intimidating at the same time.

As Millie lay in bed, she couldn't help getting giddy over the thought of seeing Walter again. She had a feeling that their connection was far from over and that there was much more to come. She closed her eyes and let herself drift off, dreaming about the possibilities that lay ahead.

As she lay there, asleep and dreaming, she was awakened by a faint knock at her window. She jumped up, heart racing, and rushed to the window, peering out into the darkness. There, in the moonlight, she saw Walter, grinning up at her.

"Care to take a walk?" he whispered.

Millie's heart leapt with joy as she nodded with excitement. Millie's heart raced as she quickly changed her clothes and rushed downstairs to meet the man of her dreams.

As she stepped outside, Walter took her hand and led her on a walk around the farm. They walked in silence for a few moments, taking in the fresh night air.

Finally, Walter broke the silence. "I can't stop thinking about you," he said, his voice barely above a whisper.

Millie's heart skipped a beat. She couldn't believe that this amazing man was interested in her. She didn't know what to say, so she just smiled shyly.

Walter continued, "There's something about you, Millie. Something that's hard to describe. But I feel like I've known you forever."

Millie felt a warmth spread through her chest. She had never felt so understood by anyone before.

As Millie and Walter walked through the fields surrounding her farm, they continued their conversation, and all of a sudden Walter asked Millie a question.

"So, Millie, what do you dream of doing with your life?" Walter asked.

Millie paused, taking a moment to gather her thoughts. "I want to see the world," she said finally. "There's so much out there beyond Simpleville, and I want to experience it all. I want to see different cultures, taste new foods, hear new music, and just soak in everything the world has to offer."

Walter smiled at her. "That's a fantastic dream, Millie. I have no doubt that you'll make it happen."

Millie was grateful for his support. "What about you, Walter? What are your goals?"

Walter's expression turned serious as he thought for a moment. "My goal is to save the world," he said finally.

Millie was taken aback. "Save the world from what?"

Walter hesitated for a moment before changing the subject. "Tell me more about your dreams, Millie. Where would you go first if you could travel anywhere?"

Millie took the hint and continued talking excitedly about her travel plans. She talked about how she wanted nothing more than to see all 32 states, and go on a safari in the neighboring town's petting zoo. Walter laughed at her enthusiasm and listened intently as she described her desire to see the world beyond their small town.

Millie then mentioned that she had a secret goal to ride a horse across the desert like a princess. Walter raised an eyebrow, amused, but didn't doubt her determination to make it happen.

Walter listened intently, nodding along and asking questions about each destination. "You have a whole world of possibilities ahead of you, Millie," he said. "I have no doubt that you'll make each of these dreams a reality."

Millie felt a rush of excitement at his words. "Thank you, Walter. You always know just what to say."

Walter smiled, taking her hand in his. "I believe in you, Millie. You can do anything you set your mind to."

As Millie and Walter continued to talk about their hopes and dreams, the night grew late and they both started to feel tired.

They walked hand in hand, their footsteps crunching on the dry grass beneath their feet. Soon they came across a large weeping willow tree, its branches stretching out wide and inviting them to rest beneath it.

Without a word, they settled down beneath the tree, leaning back against its trunk and gazing up at the twinkling stars above. The air was cool and crisp, and they wrapped their arms around each other for warmth.

As they sat there in silence, Millie couldn't help but feel a sense of peace wash over her. She had never felt so content and alive before. The world seemed to fall away around them, leaving just the two of them and the night sky.

Without a word, Walter leaned in and gently kissed her. It was a soft and sweet kiss, full of tenderness and affection. Millie's heart swelled with love for him.

They continued to kiss under the stars, lost in each other's embrace. Eventually, they grew tired and lay down, side by side, under the willow tree. They held hands as they drifted off to sleep, surrounded by the peaceful quiet of the countryside.

It was a night that Millie would never forget. She knew that Walter was someone special, and that their connection was unlike anything she had ever experienced before. As she drifted off to sleep, she couldn't wait to see what adventures lay ahead for them.

A Summer Fling To The X-Treme

Chapter 12
Up In Smoke

It was a sunny day in Simpleville, and the cool breeze blew through Walter's hair as he drove his sports car down the country road. He felt a sense of peace and tranquility being surrounded by the lush green fields and the sound of birds chirping in the distance. However, his inner thoughts were far from peaceful.

Walter was feeling remorseful about breaking his own rule of keeping his distance from Millie. He had promised himself that he wouldn't let himself get too involved with her, knowing that it could only lead to trouble. Yet, here he was, unable to resist the pull of her charm and beauty.

As he drove, he couldn't help but replay their interactions in his head. He was worried that his feelings for Millie were getting in the way of his mission. He had come to Simpleville with a purpose, and he couldn't afford to let his emotions cloud his judgment.

Walter sighed, feeling a sense of guilt wash over him. He knew he had to focus on the task at hand, but it was hard to ignore the fluttering feeling in his stomach every time he saw Millie's smile. He was lost in his thoughts, so much so that he almost missed the big black cloud of smoke in the distance.

Walter's heart skipped a beat as he saw the thick black smoke in the distance. His mind raced with the possibility that it could be coming from Samson's farm. He pushed down hard on the gas pedal, the engine of his sports car roaring as he accelerated at a frantic pace toward the source of the smoke.

The feeling of worry gnawed at him as he imagined the worst-case scenario. He couldn't shake off the thought that Samson might be in danger. His hands tightened around the steering wheel, his knuckles turning white as he navigated the car through the winding roads.

Walter's eyes remained fixated on the rising column of smoke, and he pushed the car harder, urging it to go faster.

He knew he had to get there as quickly as possible to help if he could. The adrenaline pumping through his veins kept him going, and he drove with a fierce determination to reach the farm.

Finally, he approached Samson's farm, and his heart sank at the sight of the flames engulfing the turbine. The fire was spreading rapidly, and Walter knew that he had to act fast to help Samson put it out. He brought the car to a screeching halt, jumped out, and ran toward the source of the fire.

Walter saw the turbine, the one he and Samson had built together to make smoothies, on fire. Samson was already frantically trying to put it out with a bucket of water from the creek.

"What the hell happened, Samson?" Walter asked as he rushed to help.

"I don't know," Samson replied, his voice trembling with fear as he continued to throw water onto the flaming turbine. "It was just fine, and then suddenly it just burst into flames."

Walter could feel the heat radiating from the fire, and the acrid smell of smoke filled his nostrils. He could see that the flames were too intense for them to handle with just one bucket of water.

"We need to get more water, and fast," Walter said, scanning the area for anything that could help. "Are there any hoses nearby?"

"A hose?" Samson looked at him, confused. "What is that?"

Walter's face fell. "Never mind, we'll have to think of something else."

Walter could see the panic in Samson's eyes, and he knew he had to act fast, so he grabbed a nearby bucket. "We need to keep trying, Samson. We can't let this fire destroy everything. Let's keep pouring water on it until it goes out."

Together, Walter and Samson worked frantically to try and put out the fire. Sweat poured down their faces as they poured bucket after bucket of water onto the flames. The heat was intense, and the smoke made it hard to breathe.

Walter and Samson worked tirelessly for what felt like an eternity, but eventually, their efforts paid off. The flames began to die down, and soon, the fire was out.

Exhausted and covered in sweat and soot, Walter and Samson slumped down on the ground, gasping for air.

"Thank god it's out," Samson said, wiping his brow with the back of his hand.

"Yeah," Walter replied, his heart still racing from the adrenaline. "That was intense."

The two men sat in silence for a few moments, catching their breath and processing what had just happened.

"I don't understand how it happened," Samson said finally, breaking the silence. "The turbine was working perfectly fine, and then all of a sudden, it just caught fire."

Walter and Samson walked up to the charred remains of the turbine, taking in the damage.

"I can't believe it," Samson said, shaking his head in disbelief. "We put so much work into that thing."

Walter put a comforting hand on his friend's shoulder. "I know, man. It's a real shame."

Samson turned to him, his face twisted in frustration. "What are we going to do now, Walter? We can't just give up on the smoothie business."

Walter sighed. "I know, but I don't see any way we can salvage this. The fire did too much damage."

Samson kicked at a piece of charred metal, sending it flying. "So that's it then? We're done?"

Walter put a hand on Samson's back. "No, we're not done. We'll figure something out. Maybe we can build a new one, or find another way to make smoothies."

Samson shook his head. "I don't know, man. Building that turbine was hard enough. I don't think I have it in me to start from scratch."

Walter nodded in understanding. "I get it, Samson. It's okay to feel frustrated. But we can't give up just because of one setback. We'll find a way to make this work."

Samson looked at him skeptically. "How?"

Walter noticed the pained expression on Samson's face and realized that there was more to his friend's frustration than just the fire.

"Samson, is there something else bothering you?" Walter asked gently.

Samson hesitated for a moment before letting out a heavy sigh. "It's Millie," he said finally.

"What about her?" Walter asked.

"She told me last night after the dance that she doesn't want to be with me," Samson replied, his voice barely above a whisper.

"It's not just that," Samson continued, his voice trembling. "I've had a crush on her since we were kids. And we kissed a few days ago, and I thought that maybe she felt the same way about me."

Walter stared at Samson, his mind racing with the realization that his actions had caused so much harm to those around him.

"I think I need to leave Simpleville," Walter said, his voice barely above a whisper. "I can't keep doing this, Samson. I've caused too much trouble."

"What are you talking about, Walter?" Samson asked, confused.

"I mean, look at what's happened since I got here. The turbine caught on fire, and Millie doesn't want to be with you. It's like everything I touch turns to chaos," Walter explained.

Samson shook his head. "Walter, you can't blame yourself for everything that's happened. The fire was just an accident, and Millie's decision wasn't your fault."

"But it's not just that," Walter continued, his voice growing more urgent. "I've been messing with things I shouldn't be."

Walter took a deep breath before continuing. "I need to leave on business," he blurted out.

"What business?!" Samson exclaimed, incredulous. "This was our business and now it's gone up in smoke like the rest of my life."

Walter quickly changed the subject, not wanting to get into the specifics of his mission just yet. "Listen, Samson. I know things seem tough right now, but I promise you that everything is going to work out. You just have to have a little faith."

"How can you say that?" Samson asked, his frustration evident. "Millie told me she doesn't want to be with me. And now our business is ruined. How can anything work out?"

Walter put a hand on his friend's shoulder. "I know it's hard to see right now, but trust me. I have a feeling that things are going to turn around for you. And as for the turbine, it can be rebuilt. I'll come back and help you build a new one someday. I just don't know when that will be."

Samson looked at him skeptically. "And what about you? When will you be back?"

Walter hesitated, unsure of how to answer. He didn't know when he'd be back, or if he'd be back at all. All he knew was that he had to finish his mission and save Samson and Millie from himself. "I don't know."

Walter walked toward his car, feeling the weight of the world on his shoulders. He opened the door, got in, and turned the key.

Walter's car roared to life, the engine's deep rumble echoing through the open fields. He slid on his aviator sunglasses, masking the intense emotions that churned within him. The weight of his decision to leave Simpleville now pressed heavily upon his chest, and he knew he had to go.

But Samson's question still hung in the air, lingering like a thick fog. "What business, Walter? You can't just leave me hanging like this."

Walter hesitated for a moment, then turned to face his friend. "The business of saving my world," he replied, his voice resolute.

With a heavy sigh, Walter hit the accelerator, and the car screeched backward into a spin, kicking up a cloud of dust and debris. Samson watched in stunned silence as the car tore away, leaving him standing alone.

As the car gained speed, several small pictures of watermelon, and watermelon seeds fluttered out of the open window, spiraling through the air before softly landing at Samson's feet.

Samson picked up a picture, examining it closely. The intricate details of each seed were visible, and he couldn't help but wonder why Walter had such an obsession with watermelon. The answer, however, would have to wait, as Samson was left to ponder the future without Walter, and the fate of their once-promising business venture.

A Summer Fling To The X-Treme

Chapter 13

Ashes Of Dreams

Millie slowly opened her eyes, feeling the warmth of the morning sun on her face. She sat up, rubbing the sleep from her eyes as she looked around. She was alone under the tree where she and Walter had fallen asleep.

A profound disappointment overwhelmed her as she realized he had vanished, leaving an unfillable void in her heart. Millie had enjoyed spending time with Walter, and she had hoped they could have had breakfast together or something.

Millie rose to her feet, feeling stiff from the uneven ground. As she stretched, she surveyed the peaceful forest and took in a deep breath of crisp morning air. However, something was amiss. The air had a distinct odor of burning, and it wasn't long before she noticed a thick plume of smoke in the distance, emanating from Samson's farm. The sight sent a shiver down her spine, and her heart plummeted with dread. Knowing she had to investigate, Millie hastened toward the source of the smoke.

Millie's heart raced as she ran through the fruit fields, dodging trees and bushes along the way. The closer she got to Samson's farm, the thicker the smoke became, and her worry intensified. She couldn't help but think about how Samson would react to seeing her, after she had broken his heart the night before. But she knew she had to push through her fear and make sure he was okay.

As she got closer to the farm, Millie could see the damage the fire had caused. Smoke billowed out of the ruins of Samson's water turbine, and she could see that the contraption was completely destroyed. Her heart sank even lower as she imagined how devastated Samson must be feeling. But she couldn't let that stop her.

With determination, Millie ran faster, her feet pounding on the soft earth below. As she arrived at the edge of the farm, she slowed down and cautiously approached the wreckage. She saw Samson in the distance, standing amidst the ashes, and felt a wave of relief wash over her. If he was upset to see her, at least he was okay.

As Millie approached the wreckage, she saw Samson sitting on a pile of rubble, surrounded by a pile of pictures of watermelons and watermelon seeds. His face was grim and he had tears in his eyes.

"Samson," Millie said softly, approaching him cautiously. "I'm so sorry. I just saw the smoke and ran over as fast as I could."

Samson didn't look up at her, instead he continued to stare at the pictures in his hands. "It's all gone, Millie. All of it. My water turbine and all of my equipment. Everything I've been working on for days. It's all gone."

Millie could hear the pain in his voice and she felt her own heart sink. "I'm so sorry, Samson. Is there anything I can do to help?"

Samson shook his head, "No. There's nothing anyone can do. It's all ruined. My dreams, my work, my future."

Millie didn't know what to say. She had never seen Samson so upset before, and she couldn't wrap her head around what all of the watermelon pictures were about.

Millie started to ask Samson, but he cut her off. "I don't understand how it could have happened! The turbine just burst into flames out of nowhere. One moment it was working perfectly fine, and the next thing I know, I see flames shooting out of it. All that hard work, all that time and effort, gone in a matter of seconds."

Millie watched her friend, trying to offer some comfort, but not sure what to say. She could see the frustration and anger etched on his face, and it broke her heart to see him like this. "I'm so sorry, Samson," she said softly, "but at least no one was hurt. You and Walter can always rebuild, start over again."

Samson turned to her, his eyes filled with tears. "Walter is gone."

Millie's eyes widened with confusion and fear. "Wait, what? Walter's gone? Did he... did he die in the fire?" she asked, her voice shaking.

Samson quickly shook his head. "No, no, he didn't die in the fire. He helped me put it out, and then he just up and left. No warning, nothing."

Millie didn't understand. "He's coming back though, right? He just went to get materials for a new turbine or something."

Samson looked at Millie realizing she didn't understand. "No Millie. Walter left, for good."

Millie's mind raced as she tried to process Samson's words. Walter had left town forever? She couldn't believe it. A sense of sadness washed over her, and for a moment, she didn't know what to say.

After watching her for a moment, Samson's expression turned heavy with sorrow. "I'm sorry, Millie," he said softly. It dawned on Samson that Millie didn't just not want to be with him; she wanted to be with Walter. "You really cared about him, didn't you?" he asked in a low voice.

Millie nodded slowly, tears prickling at the corners of her eyes. She had grown so used to Walter's presence in her life, and now he was just ... gone. It was hard to imagine Simpleville without him. It was hard to imagine her life without him.

"I just don't understand why he didn't say goodbye," she whispered.

Samson sighed heavily. "I don't know, Millie. I think he was just ready to move on, you know? Maybe he felt like he had nothing left for him here."

Millie's chest clenched with a sudden surge of hurt upon hearing Samson's words. "Nothing left for him here?!" she said, her voice quivering with anger now. "We had a great night together, and he just walks away without a word? That's not like him. You must have done something."

Samson furrowed his brow. "What are you talking about, Millie? I didn't do anything to Walter. He left on his own accord. Plus, if you had such a wonderful night with him, maybe you did something."

Millie crossed her arms, her eyes flashing with frustration. "Did he say anything to you before he left?"

Samson hesitated before speaking. "He said something about having to go on a business trip to save his world or something. It all sounded a bit crazy to me, to be honest."

Millie's jaw dropped. "Save the world?" That sounded familiar to her. He had mentioned that once, but it didn't seem to matter at the time. Millie looked at Samson with genuine hurt in her eyes, "Why wouldn't he tell me?"

Samson shrugged. "I don't know, Millie. Maybe he didn't want to worry you. But from the way he sped off, it seemed like it was something urgent."

Millie felt a mix of emotions. Part of her was hurt that Walter hadn't confided in her, but another part of her was proud that he was out there trying to make a difference. "I just wish he had told me," she said softly. "I feel like we could have worked it out together."

Samson put a hand on her shoulder. "I know, Millie. But maybe he'll come back someday and tell us all about his adventures."

But as Samson spoke, Millie's mind was racing. She couldn't just sit around and wait for Walter to come back. She wanted to be a part of his adventures, to help him save the world. "No," she said firmly, pushing Samson's hand off her shoulder. "I can't wait for him to come back someday. I need to go after him. I need to help him with whatever he has left town to do."

Samson's eyes widened in surprise as he heard Millie's declaration. "What? Millie, no. You can't just go running off after him like that. You have a life here, responsibilities..."

But Millie shook her head, determination etched on her face. "I have to go, Samson. I can't just sit around here wondering what could have been. Walter needs my help, and I can't just let him do this alone."

Samson knew that once Millie made up her mind, there was no talking her out of it. He let out a heavy sigh and said, "Well, if you insist on going, maybe you should take some of these with you." He gestured toward the watermelon images scattered on the ground. "They might have something to do with where Walter went. They flew out of his car as he drove away."

Millie's eyes lit up with excitement as she picked up a few of the pictures. "Thank you, Samson," she said.

Samson couldn't help but smile softly at the woman he loved. "Just promise me you'll be safe," he said, pulling her into a tight hug.

Millie hugged him back tightly. "I will. And I'll come back, Samson. I just have to do this."

With that, she pulled away from him and ran off toward the horizon, toward whatever adventures awaited her with Walter.

A Summer Fling To The X-Treme

Chapter 14
Goodbye Simpleville

Millie was determined to find Walter and nothing would stop her. She left Samson's place, went and picked up Turbo, and rode toward town. As she got closer, she saw the sign that read "Marianne's Mercantile." Millie knew she needed to stock up on supplies for the journey ahead, and this was the only store with that in town.

She entered the store, and immediately noticed the walls lined with ropes, saddles, and various other horse-riding gear. But as she made her way down the aisles, she realized that Marianne's store had much more than just horse supplies. The shelves were stocked with camping gear, survival tools, and first aid kits.

Millie couldn't help but wonder why a small store in Simpleville would have such an odd collection of items. But before she could question it, Marianne, a tough, roll-her-sleeves-up woman, appeared from behind the counter.

"What do you need?" Marianne asked, her piercing gaze assessing Millie.

Millie took a deep breath and looked around the store, taking in all the supplies. "I need to find my guy, Walter. I have to go after him, and I'll need supplies to camp overnight."

Marianne nodded knowingly. "I see. Don't worry, dear. I've got everything you need. Let's start with a tent, sleeping bag, and some cooking gear."

Marianne swiftly gathered the supplies and handed them to Millie, who was grateful for her assistance.

As Millie looked over the items, she began to feel a twinge of unease. "To be honest, Marianne, I'm not really sure what I'm doing. I've never left Simpleville before, and I don't know anything about outdoor survival."

Marianne's confident demeanor didn't falter. "Don't you worry about a thing, honey. Survival is easy once you know how. Come with me."

Marianne led Millie out back, where there was a small fire pit and targets set up for archery. She showed Millie how to build a fire, explaining the importance of kindling and how to keep the flames going.

"Now, let's work on your archery skills," Marianne said, picking up a bow and arrow. "It's a useful skill to have in the wild, and it's not as hard as you might think."

Millie was surprised by how quickly she took to the bow and arrow, hitting the targets with ease after a bit of practice. She began to feel more confident about her journey ahead, knowing that she had the supplies and skills she needed to survive in the wild.

As a long shadow cast over them, Millie realized that she needed to get going if she was going to cover any ground before dark. She turned to Marianne, "Thanks for all your help, I really appreciate it. I need to find Walter as soon as possible."

Marianne furrowed her brow in thought for a moment before exclaiming, "Wait a second. Did you say you were looking for a Walter? Walter Melone, with the sports car?"

Millie's heart leaped in her chest, "Yes! That's him. Do you know where he is?"

Marianne nodded, "I remember now. He left town a few hours ago, headed in that direction." She pointed off into the distance.

Millie mounted Turbo and turned to Marianne, "Thank you so much. You've been a lifesaver."

Marianne simply tipped her hat, "Good luck out there, Millie. And remember, you've got everything you need right here." She gestured to Millie's heart.

Millie smiled gratefully before nudging Turbo into a trot in the direction Marianne had indicated. She knew that Walter was out there somewhere, and she was determined to find him.

As Millie and Turbo rode further away from Simpleville, the terrain began to change. The lush greenery and rolling hills turned into a harsh, arid desert. The sun beat down on them relentlessly, and the wind kicked up dust that made it hard to breathe.

Days passed and the journey felt long and slow. Millie had never been on her own before, and the experience was both scary and exhilarating. She was excited to finally be leaving Simpleville, but the harsh conditions made her question if she was really cut out for this kind of adventure.

The landscape around them was barren and unforgiving, with jagged rocks and steep hillsides. Millie knew that she would need to be careful, and keep a close eye on Turbo.

The horse was her lifeline out here, and she couldn't afford to lose her.

Despite the challenges, Millie found herself growing more and more comfortable in the wilderness. She relished the freedom of the open road, and the feeling of being self-sufficient. As she rode further and further into the desert, she knew that she was on the right path, and that she would find Walter no matter what.

As the sun set over the desert, Millie dismounted her horse and set up camp. She had spent the entire day riding, and although it was exhausting, she was proud of herself for making it this far. She looked around and marveled at the beauty of the night. The sky was a deep shade of purple, with millions of stars twinkling like diamonds above her. The soft glow of the moon lit up the desert floor, casting shadows of the nearby cacti and rocks.

Millie was getting the hang of this camping thing, thanks to Marianne's guidance. She had a small fire going, and a simple tent set up. As she sat by the fire, she looked at the watermelon picture that had flown out of Walter's car. She longed to find him and be with him again. She remembered the goals they shared with each other.

Millie giggled to herself, thinking back to when she had a goal to ride through the desert like a princess. She never thought it would happen like this, alone in the desert, but it still felt magical. She imagined Walter riding beside her, holding her hand as they watched the sunset together. She wondered what he was doing at this very moment.

As she stoked the fire, Millie remembered how mysterious Walter was about his reasons for leaving. She hoped that he was safe and that he would come back to her soon. She believed that they were meant to be together, and she refused to give up on that dream.

As the night wore on, Millie stared up at the stars, lost in thought. She imagined Walter riding toward her, his car kicking up a trail of dust behind him. She could feel his arms around her, holding her tight as they watched the stars together.

In the quiet of the desert night, Millie finally drifted off to sleep, dreaming of the day she would be reunited with her love.

Recharged and love renewed, Millie packed up camp and headed out the next morning. As she rode, she saw another traveler heading toward her. As they approached, Millie could see that the traveler was a woman around her age, with a friendly smile.

"Hi there," the woman said, "My name's Lori. Where are you headed?"

"I'm looking for a man named Walter, and all he left behind was this," Millie said, holding up the watermelon picture with Florida written on the back. "Have you seen him?"

Lori shook her head. "No, sorry. But I can tell you that you're headed in the right direction. Florida's that way," she said, pointing east.

"Thanks," Millie said. "I've never been out here before, so any tips would be great."

Lori smiled. "Sure thing. I just came from Florida, actually. If you're heading that way, make sure you have plenty of water. The heat can be brutal, especially if you're not used to it."

Millie nodded, taking mental notes. "What else do I need to know?"

"Well," Lori said, "it's always good to keep an eye out for snakes and scorpions. And if you're camping out at night, make sure you have a good fire going to keep the coyotes away."

Millie thanked Lori for the tips, and the two continued chatting as they exchanged goods. Lori gave her some extra water and food, and Millie gave her a spare saddle she had picked up at Marianne's store.

"Good luck finding your man," Lori said as they parted ways.

"Thanks," Millie said, feeling grateful for the chance encounter. She rode off with renewed determination, confident that she was on the right track.

A Summer Fling To The X-Treme

Chapter 15

A Bump In The Road

Millie continued on her journey, riding through the desert for days on end. The landscape changed around her, from sand dunes to rocky cliffs to endless fields of cacti. She had never felt so alive, so free, and so focused on a goal.

As she rode, Millie thought about Walter and what he might be doing. She wondered if he was thinking about her too, and if he missed her as much as she missed him. She imagined what it would be like to finally be reunited with him, to hold him in her arms and never let go.

Despite the hardships of the journey, Millie was in good spirits. She met other travelers along the way, all with their own stories and reasons for being on the road. Some were heading south, like Millie, while others were making their way back north.

One day, Millie came across a group of travelers gathered around a campfire. They invited her to join them, and she accepted gratefully. They shared stories and songs, and Millie felt a sense of camaraderie with these strangers. They were all on their own journeys, but they were also all connected in some way.

As the night wore on, Millie found herself lost in thought once again. She thought about her life before Walter, and how it had all seemed so mundane and predictable. She thought about the day she met him, and how everything had changed in an instant. She thought about how much she had grown since embarking on this journey, and how much more she had yet to learn.

Eventually, Millie said her goodbyes to the travelers and continued on her way. She rode for several more days, always moving forward, always searching for Walter. The desert had become her home, and she had grown accustomed to its challenges and its beauty.

As Millie rode through the desert, she noticed that her horse, Turbo, had been acting a little strange. She seemed to be favoring one of her hooves, and every so often, she would let out a small whimper. Millie grew increasingly concerned as the days went by, but she didn't want to stop her journey.

Finally, one day, Millie decided to check Turbo's hooves. She dismounted and walked around to the horse's front legs, examining them closely. Sure enough, one of them was slightly swollen and had a small cut. Millie felt a pang of guilt for not noticing sooner.

She took out her first aid kit trying to tend to Turbo's injury as best she could, but it was no use. Millie knew that she didn't have the tools or expertise to fix the hoof herself. She also didn't want to risk further injury to her loyal companion. She decided to tie Turbo to a nearby tree and set out on foot to find a horse doctor in the nearest town.

After several hours of walking, Millie finally spotted a small settlement in the distance. Her heart swelled with relief as the small settlement grew closer and closer. She had been getting nervous because the scorching heat was getting to her, and her water supply was running low. As she entered the outskirts of the town, she felt a sense of hope wash over her. Perhaps there was a horse doctor nearby who could help her beloved Turbo.

As she walked down the dusty streets, Millie took in her surroundings. The town was small, with only a handful of buildings scattered around. She spotted a general store, a saloon, and a few other businesses that looked like they had seen better days. She also saw a few locals milling about, some sitting on the porch of the saloon, others lounging in the shade of a tree.

As Millie meandered through the town, she stumbled upon a sign that read "www.ASummerFl" in big, bold letters. She tilted her head in confusion, wondering what on earth it could mean. Was it some sort of secret code? Or maybe a cryptic message from the town's mysterious inhabitants? She couldn't be sure, but one thing was certain – this town was full of surprises. Maybe they spoke a different language here, or maybe they were just big fans of confusing travelers like herself. Either way, Millie couldn't think about this longer, she needed to find the horse doctor.

Approaching one of the locals, Millie politely asked if they knew of a horse doctor in the area. The man scratched his head for a moment before pointing her in the direction of a barn at the edge of town. "There's a fella named Wan who's a right good horse doctor. He should be in his barn right about now," he said.

Millie thanked the man and made her way toward the barn. Millie followed a winding dirt road that led her to the outskirts of the town. As she made her way through the dusty streets, she finally saw the large red barn off in the distance. She hurried toward it, hoping to find the horse doctor she had been searching for.

As she approached the barn, she heard the sound of horses whinnying and braying. She pushed open the creaky wooden door and stepped inside. The dimly lit interior was filled with the musky smell of hay and manure.

In the corner of the barn, she spotted a figure hunched over a workbench, tinkering with a set of horseshoes. She approached the figure and cleared her throat to get their attention. The figure turned around, revealing an older man with a grizzled beard and piercing blue eyes.

"Excuse me, sir," Millie said. "I'm looking for a horse doctor. Do you know where I might find one?"

The man nodded and gestured toward a closed door at the back of the barn. "You'll find Doctor Wan through that door," he said. "But be warned, he's a bit of a character."

With a grateful smile, Millie made her way toward the door, feeling a mix of nerves and excitement. She pushed the door open and stepped inside, unsure of what to expect.

As Millie pushed the door open, she found herself in a dimly lit room filled with hay bales and tools scattered around. She saw a man hunched over a workbench, tinkering with some metal pieces.

The man turned around at the sound of the door opening and looked at Millie with a curious expression. He was a kind looking man with a wise face, dressed in a worn leather apron.

"Hello there," he said in a calm voice. "What brings you to my humble abode?"

Millie stepped forward and introduced herself, explaining her situation with Turbo's injured hoof. Doctor Wan listened intently, nodding along and occasionally grunting in acknowledgment.

Once Millie finished her explanation, Doctor Wan stroked his beard thoughtfully and said, "Well, let's not waste any time then. Lead the way, young lady."

Millie led the way out of the barn and toward where she had left Turbo. As they rode, Doctor Wan asked her about her journey and where she was headed.

"I'm looking for the love of my life," Millie explained. "He went missing, and I'm trying to find him."

Doctor Wan raised an eyebrow. "Sounds like quite the adventure," he said with a chuckle. "I'm sure you'll find him soon enough."

Millie smiled, grateful for the doctor's kindness and encouragement. They arrived at Turbo's side, and Doctor Wan got to work assessing the horse's injury.

After a few moments, Dr. Wan straightened up and turned to Millie. "I'm afraid your horse will need to stay in the barn for a couple of nights," he said. "The wound isn't serious, but it will require some care and attention to heal properly."

Millie felt a twinge of disappointment at the news. She had been eager to continue her journey toward Walter, but she knew that Turbo's health was more important. "What can I do to help her?" she asked the doctor.

Dr. Wan smiled kindly at her. "Well, we'll need to clean the wound and bandage it properly," he said. "And your horse will need to stay off her feet for a while to give the injury time to heal."

Millie nodded, feeling grateful for the doctor's help. "Thank you, Dr. Wan," she said. "I'll do whatever it takes to make sure Turbo is healthy again."

The doctor patted her on the shoulder. "Don't worry, my dear," he said. "I'll take good care of her. You just focus on getting some rest and come back in a few days to check on her."

Millie felt a wave of exhaustion wash over her as she left the barn. She knew she couldn't leave Turbo alone in the care of Dr. Wan, but she also needed a place to rest for the night.

She walked through the streets of the small town, scanning the buildings for any signs of an inn or lodging. As she walked, she passed by a few locals who gave her curious looks. She realized she must have stood out as an outsider in this close-knit community. She wondered if this is what Walter felt like when he first showed up in Simpleville.

After a few minutes of wandering, she finally spotted a small inn called "The Rusty Spur". She breathed a sigh of relief and made her way inside.

The innkeeper, a friendly-looking woman with graying hair, greeted her warmly. "Welcome to The Rusty Spur, dearie. What can I do for you?"

Millie explained her situation and asked if there was a room available for her to stay in while her horse recovered. The innkeeper nodded sympathetically and led her to a small but cozy room at the back of the inn.

"There you are, dearie," she said, gesturing to the bed. "Make yourself at home. And if you need anything, just give me a holler."

Millie thanked her and collapsed onto the bed, feeling the weariness of her journey catching up with her. As she drifted off to sleep, she couldn't help but wonder what the next few days would bring.

A Summer Fling To The X-Treme

A Summer Fling To The X-Treme

Chapter 16
Cooking With Watermelon

The next day Millie strolled through the small town, marveling at the quaintness of it all. She had seen so much of the country already, but there was something special about this place. As she walked, she spotted a small library nestled in between two buildings. The sight of it made her heart flutter with excitement.

She pushed the door open and was greeted by a musty smell and the creaking sound of the old wooden floorboards. She scanned the room, taking in the rows upon rows of books stacked from floor to ceiling. The library was small, but cozy.

As she walked along the shelves, she wondered if they had a section on watermelons. She couldn't help but wonder why Walter had so many pictures of them. She reached out to touch the spine of random books, wondering if there was anything in there that could shed light on the matter.

Just then, a voice called out to her from behind the desk. "Can I help you find something?" the librarian asked.

Millie turned to face the source of the voice and saw a kind-looking woman sitting behind a desk, a smile on her lips. "Actually, I was just curious about watermelons," Millie replied, making her way over to the desk.

Millie gazed at the librarian, taking in her bushy red hair and big tortoiseshell glasses. There was something about the woman that made her feel at ease. The librarian stood up and walked around the desk, her steps light and airy.

"Meggan," she said, extending a hand toward Millie. "I'm the librarian here. And you're interested in watermelons, huh?" Meggan's eyes twinkled mischievously behind her glasses.

Millie couldn't help but smile at the librarian's friendly demeanor. "Yes, I saw this section and I just had to know more. Do you have any recommendations?"

Meggan's smile grew wider. "Oh, do I ever! Let me show you the best of the bunch." She led Millie toward the watermelon section, chatting merrily as they walked. As they passed a sign that read "ingToTheXTreme", Millie couldn't help but feel a pang of curiosity. What could that possibly mean?

Meggan pointed Millie toward a few books on watermelon and then excused herself to attend to another patron. Millie was left alone with the books, her curiosity piqued. She browsed through the titles, taking note of some of the interesting ones.

One title caught her eye: "The Health Benefits of Watermelon: Beyond Hydration." She pulled it off the shelf and flipped through the pages. The book was filled with fascinating facts about watermelon and its many benefits. Did you know that watermelon is an excellent source of vitamin C and contains lycopene, a powerful antioxidant? Millie certainly didn't.

She also picked up "The History and Culture of Watermelon," and "Cooking with Watermelon." After reading through a few sections, she realized just how much she didn't know about the fruit. She was impressed with its versatility and how it could be used in sweet and savory dishes alike.

Although Millie still didn't have any answers about Walter's watermelon obsession, she did gain a newfound appreciation for the fruit's refreshing and hydrating nature.

Millie continued reading "Cooking with Watermelon" and found herself drawn in by the creative recipes and uses for the fruit. She made a mental note to try some of them out in her own cooking.

After a while, Millie decided to bring the book back to the front desk and chat with Meggan. "This is a great collection of watermelon books you have here," Millie said, smiling at the librarian.

Meggan's face lit up. "Oh, thank you! I'm so glad you're enjoying it. A lot of them go unread, but that's actually the second time this week someone has read it."

Millie's ears perked up. "Really? Who else has been reading about watermelons?"

Meggan thought for a moment before answering. "Let's see ... he was a gentleman who drove a sports car. I believe his name was ...Walt, Walter, something like that."

Millie's heart began to race. "Did he happen to mention where he was headed?" she asked, hoping for any clue.

Meggan shook her head. "I'm sorry, dear, but all I know was that he was headed to the next town over. He was just passing through town and stopped by the library to do some research. He seemed quite interested in watermelons."

Millie's mind raced. "Thank you so much, Meggan!" she exclaimed. "You've been incredibly helpful."

Millie practically ran out of the library, eager to continue her search for Walter. She made her way down the street to the horse doctor's office. As she burst through the door, Doctor Wan looked up from his desk, surprised by her sudden entrance.

"Is Turbo ready to go?" Millie asked Doctor Wan, her eyes shining with excitement.

Doctor Wan smiled warmly at Millie. "Yes, she's all healed up and ready for the road. Just be sure to keep an eye on that foot, and don't push her too hard."

Millie nodded eagerly. "I will. Thank you, Doctor Wan! I'm off to find Walter!" With that, she quickly mounted Turbo and rode off toward the horizon, her heart full of hope and determination.

A Summer Fling To The X-Treme

Chapter 17

A Broken Crystal Ball

Millie and Turbo took a slow trot down the dusty road, the sun beating down on their backs. Turbo was eager to run, to stretch her legs and feel the wind in her hair, but Millie held her back. She remembered Doctor Wan's advice to take it easy on Turbo, to let her get used to the open road and to the long rides.

As they made their way toward the neighboring town, Millie felt a sense of unease that she couldn't quite put her finger on. She had been to many small towns on her travels, but this one felt different somehow. It was as if the town was hiding something, and the people were guarding a secret.

As she went from person to person, asking about the red sports car, she started to get frustrated. No one seemed to have seen it, or at least, no one was willing to admit they had seen it. She wondered if the townspeople were lying to her, or if they were simply trying to protect their own.

As she talked to the people of the town, she noticed that they were a little less friendly and more standoffish than people in other towns she had visited. They seemed guarded and suspicious, as if they didn't want to reveal too much about themselves or their town.

Millie tried to keep a positive attitude, but the lack of progress was starting to get to her. She loved Walter deeply, and the thought of losing him was almost unbearable. She couldn't help but wonder what could have happened to him, and why he would have disappeared without a trace.

Despite her frustration and the town's mysterious vibe, Millie soldiered on, determined to find any information that could lead her to Walter.

Millie decided to try her luck at the local saloon in the neighboring town. She tied up Turbo outside and headed inside, scanning the dimly lit room for any sign of Walter.

She made her way to the bar and struck up a conversation with the bartender.

"Excuse me, have you seen a man by the name of Walter around here?" Millie asked hopefully.

The bartender shook his head. "Can't say that I have, miss."

Millie sighed, feeling the weight of disappointment settling in her chest. She was about to leave when she felt a tap on her shoulder. She turned to find a woman with a glossy mane of sleek straight hair and a mischievous smile.

"Did I overhear you asking about a man named Walter?" the woman asked.

Millie nodded, intrigued by the stranger's boldness. "Yes, I have. Do you know something about him?"

The woman leaned in, her eyes glittering with excitement. "I might. Why don't you come back to my shop and we can discuss it over a cup of tea?"

Millie hesitated for a moment. She had learned to be cautious on her travels, especially when it came to strangers. But there was something about this woman that made her curious. She made a split-second decision and followed the woman out of the saloon.

As they walked down the street, Millie couldn't help but notice the woman's easy confidence and carefree attitude.

She seemed to radiate a sense of mystery and coolness that Millie found both alluring and intimidating.

Finally, they arrived at the woman's shop, a cozy little space filled with eclectic trinkets and colorful fabrics. The woman, who introduced herself as the Amazing Avery, ushered Millie to a table and poured them each a cup of steaming tea.

"I must say, Millie, I sense a great deal of eagerness and desire in you," Avery said, eyeing Millie over her tea cup.

Millie felt a sudden rush of unease. She wasn't sure if she was comfortable with a complete stranger knowing so much about her. But at the same time, she couldn't deny that she was desperate for any information about Walter.

"How did you know?" Millie asked, trying to sound nonchalant.

"I have a way of sensing people's wants and needs," Avery replied cryptically. "And I can help you find what you're looking for, Millie. But first, I will show the thing you want most in life."

With that, Avery pulled out a crystal ball from under the table and began to gaze into it intently. Millie watched, fascinated, as the colors swirled and danced within the ball. She had never believed in psychics or crystal balls before, but something about Avery made her want to believe.

"What do you see?" Millie asked, leaning in closer.

Avery takes a deep breath and stares into the crystal ball. Millie leans in closer, her heart pounding with anticipation.

"I saw a man," Avery said slowly, her voice filled with confidence.

"Is it Walter?" Millie asked eagerly.

But Avery shook her head. "No, it's not Walter. It's someone else."

Millie felt a pang of disappointment, but she urged Avery to continue.

"I saw you and this man ... you were laughing and holding hands together. You were married and looked so happy," Avery said, her voice growing even more confident.

Millie's mind raced as she tried to imagine who this man could be. She felt a sudden jolt of hope, thinking that if it wasn't Walter, it must be Samson. They had some magical moments, but she had been pushing him away in her single-minded pursuit of Walter.

Avery's words stirred something inside Millie, a sense of longing and regret. Could it be that she had been chasing after the wrong man this whole time? She tried to push aside the image of Samson and focused on her love for Walter.

"No, that can't be it," Millie told Avery, determined to find Walter.

Avery looked surprised by Millie's response.

"Oh. Okay," she said, taking the crystal ball in her hands once again. She shook it, then gazed into it with renewed confidence. This time, she saw something different. "I saw his car," Avery said excitedly. "It was parked on the side of the road. And I saw Walter in a watermelon field, inspecting the fruit."

"Can you tell me how to find him?" Millie asked eagerly.

Avery smiled knowingly. "You're close," she said. "Just follow your heart. It won't take you longer than a day to find him."

Millie nodded, feeling a renewed sense of hope. "Thank you," she said, rising from her seat. "I won't forget your kindness."

But as she started to get up from the chair, Avery pulled her back into the seat. "Wait," she said, closing her eyes and concentrating. "I'm getting a third vision, a final sign."

Millie settled back into the chair, watching as Avery shook the crystal ball again. After a few moments, Avery's eyes snapped open, and she looked at Millie with a puzzled expression. ".com/TRULUVFND," she said. "Does that mean anything to you?"

Millie furrowed her brow. "Ummm no, but that other stuff was super helpful," she said, confused by the seemingly random vision.

Avery shrugged, looking a bit disappointed. "Well, maybe it'll make sense to you later," she said.

As Millie left the shop, she felt a sense of purpose. She knew that she was on the right track now, and that she would find Walter soon. She returned to Turbo, ready to hit the road once again.

A Summer Fling To The X-Treme

Chapter 18
The Truth Revealed

Millie followed her heart like the Amazing Avery had told her, and she finally arrived in Florida. The warmth of the sun and the soft sandy beaches were a stark contrast to the rugged terrain and ever-changing weather she had encountered during her long journey on horseback. She felt a wave of relief and joy wash over her as she realized that she had finally made it to her destination.

Millie's faithful horse, who had carried her all the way across the country, neighed happily as they reached the outskirts of the small town where she hoped the watermelon field would be. She patted Turbo's neck affectionately, grateful for her unwavering loyalty and endurance throughout the long journey.

As she rode into town, Millie couldn't help but feel a sense of excitement and wonder at the new adventures that lay ahead. She had dreamed of coming to Florida ever since she knew Walter might be heading there, and now that she was finally here, she felt like anything was possible.

Millie looked around at the vibrant colors and sounds of the town, and she knew that this was just the beginning of her new chapter. She was ready to embrace all the beauty and challenges that lay ahead, as long as Walter would be by her side.

All of a sudden, Millie was struck by the sight of hundreds of round, plump watermelons dotting the landscape. The watermelon field she had been searching for stretched out before her as far as the eye could see, with rows upon rows of green vines and leaves trailing in every direction.

The sun was high in the sky, casting a warm glow over the scene, and the gentle breeze carried the sweet, tangy scent of ripe watermelon to Millie's nose. She felt her mouth water with anticipation, and couldn't help but let out a small sigh of pleasure at the sight.

As she drew closer to the field, Millie could see workers moving among the rows, picking and sorting the melons with practiced ease. Their movements were fluid and graceful, almost like a dance, and the sight of them working in harmony with the land filled Millie with a sense of awe and respect.

For a moment, she simply sat on her horse and watched, taking in the beauty of the scene before her. It was a moment of pure bliss, of feeling at one with the world around her, and she knew that she would remember it always.

As Millie rode through the watermelon field, she couldn't help but feel a sense of wonder at the vastness of it all. The bright green leaves of the watermelon vines stretched out in all directions, and the sweet smell of ripening fruit filled the air.

As Millie rode through the field, her heart began to race with anticipation. She had traveled across the entire country to find Walter, and now she was finally here, in the heart of Florida, where she knew he was supposed to be on this watermelon farm. According to the psychic at least.

As she scanned the field, her eyes were immediately drawn to a tall figure standing in the distance. Even from this far away, she could tell it was Walter. She felt a jolt of electricity run through her body, and she urged her horse to gallop toward him.

The wind whipped through her hair as she rode across the vast expanse of watermelon plants, her heart pounding in her chest. The closer she got, the more details she could make out about Walter. She could see his bright red shirt he always wore with his green pants, and the way his hair fell across his forehead in messy waves.

Finally, she reached him, and their eyes locked in a moment of pure, unadulterated joy. Walter's face lit up with a huge smile as he took in the sight of Millie riding toward him. He dropped the watermelon he had been holding and began to run toward her.

As they met in the middle of the field, Millie leapt from her horse and threw her arms around Walter's neck, burying her face in his chest. He wrapped his arms tightly around her, pulling her close, and they stood there for what felt like an eternity, lost in the moment.

Finally, they pulled back, and Walter looked into Millie's eyes, his voice choked with emotion. "I can't believe you're here," he said. "I've missed you so much."

Millie could feel tears welling up in her own eyes as she gazed at him, her heart bursting with love. "I had to come find you," she said. "I couldn't stand being away from you any longer."

As they stood there, holding each other in the middle of the watermelon field, Millie knew that everything was going to be alright. She had found the love of her life, and she would never let him go.

Suddenly Millie felt Walter pull away. As she looked up at him his expression had turned serious.

"Walter, what's wrong?" Millie asked, her heart racing.

"Millie, there's something I need to tell you," Walter replied, his voice solemn.

Millie's heart sank as she sensed the gravity of Walter's words. She braced herself for whatever he was about to say, her mind racing with possibilities.

"Walter, whatever it is, you can tell me," Millie said, trying to remain calm.

Walter took a deep breath before speaking. "Millie, I know I should have told you before, but I've been keeping something from you. And since you've come all this way, I think you deserve the truth."

Millie's eyes widened as she processed Walter's words. "What do you mean? You've been lying to me?"

"Something like that," Walter said, looking away for a moment before meeting Millie's gaze once more. "Millie, I'm not from this time. I'm actually from the future."

Millie's mind reeled as she tried to make sense of what Walter just said. "The future? What are you talking about?"

Walter took a deep breath before continuing. "I know it's hard to believe, but it's true. I came back in time to plant a seed, and well to find some seeds too. And I never intended to fall in love with you, but I did."

Millie felt a mix of emotions wash over her. Confusion, disbelief, but also a glimmer of hope. "What do you mean, plant seeds? Find seeds? You're not making any sense Walter."

Walter's expression darkened. "It's complicated, but let's just say that the future I come from is having some issues. And I came back to try and fix it."

Millie looked at Walter, as she tried to read his expression. "And you didn't think to tell me any of this before now?"

"I didn't want to burden you with it," Walter said, his tone apologetic. "But now that you're here, I can't keep it from you any longer. I'll explain everything."

With a mixture of anticipation and trepidation, Millie gestured to her horse, "Hop on," she said, her voice filled with a mix of determination and curiosity. "We have a lot to talk about."

Walter hesitated for a moment, looking at Turbo's back as if contemplating the idea. Then, with a resolute nod, he stepped forward and swiftly climbed onto the back of the horse behind Millie. Their bodies pressed together, and

Millie could feel the warmth of Walter's presence as he wrapped his arms around her waist for stability.

"Hold on tight," Millie advised, her voice tinged with excitement as she gently nudged Turbo forward. The horse responded with a swift, fluid motion, carrying them away from the vast watermelon field and toward a secluded spot where Walter could reveal the secrets he had been keeping.

As they rode, the wind whipped through Millie's hair, adding an exhilarating sensation to the moment. The rhythmic sound of Turbo's hooves on the ground created a comforting cadence that echoed their shared journey.

In this intimate embrace on horseback, Millie couldn't help but feel a deep connection with Walter, as if their souls were entwined in this pivotal moment. The world around them blurred, and the focus narrowed down to their intertwined destinies.

Walter's gaze softened as he locked eyes with Millie, the weight of his revelation evident in his expression. The quiet clearing provided a sense of intimacy and safety, enveloping them in a cocoon of shared secrets.

"Millie," Walter began, his voice filled with a mix of earnestness and vulnerability. "I owe you the truth, no matter how extraordinary it may sound. You see, I traveled back in time because there was a crucial task I needed to accomplish."

Millie's brows furrowed slightly, her curiosity piqued. She took a step closer to Walter, their bodies instinctively gravitating toward each other. "What is it, Walter?" she asked, her voice a gentle encouragement.

Walter took a deep breath, collecting his thoughts before continuing. "I traveled back in time to teach Samson about the wonders of smoothies and the magic of blending fruits, creating delicious concoctions."

Millie's eyes widened, a mixture of surprise and intrigue dancing within them. The notion seemed surreal, yet she could sense the sincerity in Walter's voice.

"You see, Millie," Walter continued, his words flowing with conviction, "Samson's great grandson, inspired by the knowledge he gained from my teachings, went on to establish a successful chain of smoothie stores in the future. Those stores would eventually become known as Smoothie King, an empire built upon the very essence of clean ingredients and desirable taste."

Millie stood there, absorbing the weight of Walter's words. It was an extraordinary revelation, one that surpassed the boundaries of her imagination. Yet, in the depths of her heart, she could feel the resonance of truth.

"I traveled through time, risking everything, because the impact of Samson's great grandson's creation will have far-reaching consequences," Walter explained, his gaze never leaving Millie's face. "Smoothie King will touch countless lives, promoting healthy lifestyles and becoming a beacon of wellness in the future."

A sense of wonderment washed over Millie as she contemplated the significance of the mission. It was a grand tapestry woven through time, where the simplest of actions could shape the course of history. She knew that Samson would be thrilled to hear that his life would have so much meaning to so many people.

"I understand, Walter," Millie finally spoke, her voice filled with a mixture of awe and determination. "But what I still don't get is why you left? And why did you leave for a watermelon field?"

Walter's eyes held a gentle sincerity as he listened to Millie's words, her curiosity and genuine desire for understanding shining through. He knew he had to share the full extent of his mission, the gravity of his purpose, with the woman he had fallen for.

"Millie," Walter began, his voice filled with a mix of gratitude and determination. "You're right, there is another reason why I came back in time, and it relates to the watermelon field."

Millie's brows furrowed in confusion, her gaze fixed on Walter, eager for his explanation.

Proudly for a moment, Walter said, "You see, in my time period, I am the inventor of the X-Treme Watermelon Smoothie from Smoothie King."

"Wow. That sounds really delicious and important." Millie said.

Walter continued, "Well you see there is a problem though. The summers have become unbearably hot in my time, Millie. People are so thirsty it's disturbing."

Millie tried to imagine such a thirst, but she couldn't.

"The X-Treme Watermelon Smoothie has become the number one way for people to quench their thirst in the summertime." Walter shared.

Millie, surprised and excited, said, "Well that's wonderful Walter! You must be so proud."

"I would be if it weren't for the fact that watermelon seeds are on the brink of extinction," Walter revealed, his voice laced with a touch of sadness. "The delicate balance of nature has been disrupted, and watermelon plants struggle to produce viable seeds. If we don't intervene, future generations will never know the hydrating magic of sipping an X-Treme Watermelon Smoothie from Smoothie King."

Millie's eyes widened with a mix of astonishment and concern. The thought of a world without mouth-puckering smoothies seemed unfathomable, and she realized the weight of the task that lay before them.

"I couldn't let that happen, Millie," Walter continued, his voice tinged with determination. "So, part of my mission was to find watermelon seeds in this time period, where they are still abundant and thriving. I needed to gather as many seeds as possible and bring them back to our time, to safeguard their existence and preserve the legacy of Smoothie King."

Millie stood there, a profound sense of purpose and responsibility washing over her. The significance of their journey, the intertwining of their love and the fate of watermelons, was a realization that humbled her.

"Walter, it's incredible," she finally spoke, her voice filled with a blend of awe and determination. "To think that our love not only spans time but is also intricately connected to the preservation of something so simple yet so essential as watermelon seeds."

A soft smile graced Walter's lips, filled with gratitude and love.

A Summer Fling To The X-Treme

Chapter 19

A Decision For All

Hours had passed since Walter had revealed the truth of his extraordinary mission to Millie. They sat together in the cozy warmth of the clearing, their conversation stretching into the depths of the night. The weight of their words hung in the air, mingling with a mix of emotions that danced within their hearts.

As the moon cast its soft glow upon them, Walter's gaze fell upon Millie, his eyes filled with a blend of remorse and affection. The magnitude of his actions, the ripples they had caused in her life, weighed heavily on his conscience.

"Millie," he whispered, his voice tinged with regret. "I want to apologize. I never intended for all of this to happen. I never meant to create such a mess, to complicate your life like this."

Millie's eyes met his, her expression a tapestry of understanding and compassion. She reached out, gently placing her hand on his, her touch a reassuring warmth.

"Walter," she spoke softly, her voice laced with tenderness. "You have nothing to apologize for. The heart follows its own path, and sometimes, no matter how much we try to resist, feelings take hold. We can't control that."

A flicker of hope ignited within Walter's eyes as he absorbed her words. The love he had discovered in Millie's presence had shaken his resolve, upending his original intentions. Her return had reignited a spark within him, a longing to remain in this time, by her side.

"But Millie," Walter's voice quivered, uncertainty tainting his words. "I have to admit that now that you're back, I find myself reconsidering my decision to return to the future. My heart yearns for a life with you, a future that we can build together."

Millie's heart skipped a beat, her breath catching in her throat. Walter's vulnerability, his confession, awakened a whirlwind of emotions within her. The idea of a shared future, a life intertwined with his, ignited a flame of possibility in her soul.

Millie's mind began to wander, painting vivid images of what their life could be like if Walter stayed in her time. In the depths of her imagination, she wove a tapestry of dreams and possibilities, each stroke of her thoughts bringing their shared future to life.

She envisioned mornings filled with gentle sunlight streaming through the curtains of their cozy farmhouse, where Walter's presence would be a constant source of warmth and comfort. They would wake up to the soft melodies of birdsong, savoring the simple joys of a shared breakfast at a table adorned with freshly picked flowers.

In her mind's eye, she saw them strolling hand in hand through lush meadows, their laughter mingling with the fragrance of wildflowers. They would explore the wonders of nature together, discovering hidden trails and secret hideaways, their hearts overflowing with a sense of adventure.

Millie imagined evenings spent nestled in front of a crackling fireplace, their bodies entwined, lost in intimate conversations that spanned the breadth of their lives. They would share their hopes, their dreams, and their deepest fears, finding solace and strength in the unwavering support of their connection.

In her visions, she saw them embarking on grand journeys together, traveling to far-off lands and immersing themselves in diverse cultures. They would marvel at ancient ruins, sample exotic cuisines, and create memories that would forever be etched in their souls.

Millie's thoughts wandered to moments of shared laughter, stolen kisses, and the tender embrace of a love that grew deeper with each passing day. She envisioned Walter's eyes sparkling with joy as they danced beneath a moonlit sky, their bodies swaying to the rhythm of their own love story.

But above all, Millie imagined a future filled with unwavering love and unwavering support. She pictured Walter by her side, weathering life's storms together, celebrating triumphs and offering solace in times of sorrow. Their love would be a steadfast anchor, a guiding light illuminating their path through the ebbs and flows of existence.

As Millie's thoughts meandered through the realm of possibilities, she couldn't help but consider the repercussions of Walter's choice to stay in her time period. The impact reverberated beyond their own lives, extending to the future that Walter hailed from. She imagined a world where the absence of Walter's presence would leave a void, altering the course of events and transforming the lives of countless individuals.

She saw a future devoid of the vibrant energy that Smoothie King had infused into the world. The absence of

X-Treme Watermelon Smoothies, crafted with Walter's expertise, left a void in the lives of people craving a refreshing and healthy indulgence. The magic of those smoothies had become a staple, a source of nourishment, and a symbol of rejuvenation for many.

Millie imagined individuals, once vibrant and full of vitality, grappling with the absence of that flavorful elixir. The people who relied on the daily boost of energy and hydration found themselves searching for alternatives, yearning for the familiar taste and the rejuvenating effects that only Walter's smoothies could provide.

She envisioned parched throats and weary bodies, longing for the invigorating rush of watermelon-infused bliss that had become a trademark of Walter's creations. The absence of that simple pleasure weighed heavy on the hearts and souls of those in the future, creating a void that could not easily be filled.

Millie's thoughts drifted to the athletes who once relied on the nourishing smoothies to fuel their performance who found themselves searching for a substitute, their bodies and minds yearning for the revitalizing boost that Walter's concoctions provided. The absence of that essential component disrupted routines, altering the trajectory of their athletic endeavors.

She imagined individuals who had found solace in the wholesome goodness of the smoothies, relying on them to maintain their health and wellness. The absence of Walter's creations left them longing for the nutritional balance they had come to depend upon, leaving a void that no other meal could adequately fill.

The future she envisioned portrayed a world where the absence of Walter's expertise in the realm of smoothies cast a shadow over the lives of many. It was a reality where the sweetness of watermelon and the mastery of blending had become a lost art, leaving people yearning for a taste they would never experience again.

As Millie pondered the implications, her heart weighed heavily with a sense of responsibility. She understood the magnitude of the decision before Walter, recognizing that the choice to stay would alter the lives of many in his time period. It was a decision that held the power to shape the future, to either preserve the legacy of Smoothie King or allow it to fade into oblivion.

With a deep breath and determination in her eyes, Millie's imagination turned into a resolve. She knew that the consequences were vast, and the responsibility immense.

She took a moment to gather her thoughts, her gaze locked with Walter's.

As the weight of the decision hung in the air, Millie mustered the courage to express her thoughts to Walter. She understood the magnitude of his mission and the impact his presence had in the future. Taking a deep breath, she looked into his eyes and spoke with a mixture of love and selflessness.

"Walter," she began, her voice steady but filled with emotion. "I can't deny the depth of my feelings for you, the way you've touched my heart in ways I never thought possible. If you choose to stay, to be here with me, I wouldn't want to stop you, but I know that it wouldn't be the right thing to do. We can't ignore the greater purpose that brought you here. The future needs you, Walter. Your knowledge, your skills, and the impact of Smoothie King on people's lives—it's something that shouldn't be sacrificed."

Walter listened intently, his gaze locked with Millie's. He could sense the sincerity and selflessness in her words, and a mixture of emotions flickered across his face. His heart ached at the thought of leaving Millie behind, but he also knew the gravity of his mission and the potential consequences of abandoning it.

Millie continued, her voice filled with conviction. "The world needs the X-Treme Watermelon Smoothies, Walter. It's not just about us—it's about the countless lives that will be impacted by the happiness and hydration they provide. If you stay here, we might have a beautiful life together, but it could come at the cost of a future where those people won't have access to what they need."

Walter's eyes softened as he absorbed Millie's words. He realized that she was right, and that his personal desires had to be set aside for the greater good. The weight of responsibility settled upon him, and he knew deep down what he needed to do.

With a mix of gratitude and sadness, Walter reached out and gently held Millie's hands. "Millie," he said, his voice filled with a mix of love and determination, "you have shown me the depth of your selflessness and the magnitude of your love. I can't thank you enough for understanding and supporting me in this decision. The world needs the X-Treme Watermelon Smoothies, and I must fulfill my mission."

Tears welled up in Millie's eyes as she nodded, her heart filled with love and admiration for Walter. She knew it wouldn't be easy to let him go, but she also recognized the importance of his purpose. They shared a bittersweet embrace, cherishing the time they had together, even if it was just a limited-time summer fling.

As they stood there, intertwined in each other's arms, Walter whispered words of love and gratitude to Millie, assuring her that their connection would endure, despite the distance and the passage of time. With a final, lingering gaze, Walter reluctantly pulled away from their embrace, his heart heavy but resolute.

Millie looked at Walter and said, "I have one last way to help you." Millie and Walter both mounted Turbo once again and rode back to the watermelon fields.

Hand in hand, they ventured into the watermelon field once again, their purpose renewed. Together, they would gather the precious seeds, carefully preserving them for the journey back to Walter's time.

As they worked side by side, their shared passion and commitment breathed life into each delicate seed they collected. They knew that the act of saving these seeds was more than a preservation of a fruit; it was an act of hope, a testament to the power of love and the resilience of nature.

With every seed collected, Millie and Walter felt a renewed sense of purpose, their hearts intertwining with the destiny of the watermelon seeds. They knew that their journey together would soon be ending, but the legacy they would leave behind would ripple through time, touching the lives of future generations.

Together, they would ensure that the taste of summer, the simple pleasure of a juicy X-Treme Watermelon Smoothie, would endure, allowing future generations to experience the same joy and delight that had brought Millie and Walter together.

And as they stood amidst the watermelon field, their hands clasped tightly, they knew that love, determination, and the power of a shared mission could defy the boundaries of time itself.

A Summer Fling To The X-Treme

Chapter 20

Back In The Right Time

Walter stood in awe as he gazed around the enormous greenhouse filled with rows and rows of watermelons, stretching as far as the eye could see. The vibrant green leaves of the watermelon plants and the deep red hue of the fruit were a sight to behold.

Walter couldn't help but marvel at the unforeseen outcomes of his journey to the past.

When Walter had set out on his mission to collect watermelon seeds, he had hoped for success, but deep down, he had carried a seed of doubt. The future he had left behind was a parched landscape, where people struggled to quench their thirst amidst scorching summers. It was a world on the brink of crisis, with watermelon seeds on the verge of extinction.

But now, as he looked around, he realized that his efforts had borne fruit—quite literally.
Walter's heart swelled with a mix of astonishment and pride. His mission, once deemed impossible, had become a reality. The simple act of collecting watermelon seeds from the past had brought about a significant change in the future. His invention of The X-Treme Watermelon Smoothie had become a sensation, satisfying the seemingly unquenchable thirst of the people in his time.

The X-Treme Watermelon Smoothie had become a lifeline for people in the scorching summers, providing them with much-needed hydration and relief.

As he reflected on the magnitude of his achievement, a sense of wonder enveloped Walter. He had traveled back in time to Simpleville and befriended Samson, helping him to invent the smoothie and ensuring the creation of Smoothie King in the future. Throughout his travels, meeting Samson, and Millie, he faced countless challenges, and overcame adversity, all in the pursuit of a better future.

In that moment, Walter realized that he had played a small but pivotal role in shaping the world. The future was no longer a bleak and desolate place, but a realm of possibilities and promise. And as he basked in the surprising outcomes of his travels, a newfound determination ignited within him—a resolve to continue making a difference, one seed at a time.

As he marveled at the scene, a familiar hand was placed on his shoulder. He turned around to see his superior, Mr. McCracken, standing behind him with a big smile on his face.

"Well done, Walter!" Mr. McCracken exclaimed, "You've saved the world, my boy!"

Mr. McCracken noticed the look of pride on Walter's face and patted him on the back. "You deserve it, son. You've worked tirelessly to ensure the survival of our world. You are a true hero."

Walter forced a smile, but his heart was heavy. The world may have been saved, but it had come at a cost. Millie, the love of his life, had stayed behind in the past. She had understood him in a way that no one else did, and he couldn't help but wonder if he would ever see her again.

As he pondered, Mr. McCracken continued. "Thanks to The X-Treme Watermelon Smoothie, the world has quenched its thirst, and the effects have been remarkable. The people of our time have become hydrated, in an incredibly unique and fulfilling way. They have used their newfound energy to accomplish incredible feats. The X-Treme Watermelon Smoothie helped the world beat the summer heat, just in time for fall!"

Walter's eyes widened in amazement. "That's incredible, sir."

"Yes, it is," Mr. McCracken agreed. "But now, we must turn our attention to the future. There are others out there who need your help, Walter. Are you ready for the next adventure?"

Walter took a deep breath, feeling a renewed sense of purpose. "I'm ready, sir. Where to next?"

Mr. McCracken smiled mischievously. "One word. Pumpkin."

As the summers passed by, Walter had become somewhat of a celebrity in his own time, with accolades and honors bestowed upon him for his contribution to saving the world from thirst. But with all the fanfare and attention, he found himself longing for a simpler life.

As the years passed, Walter grew restless and yearned for something more than just the endless cycle of work and praise. He longed for personal fulfillment, for a deeper connection that went beyond just his achievements.

And then one fall day, Walter met Lillie. She was a small town girl, with an infectious laugh and a smile that lit up the room. Unlike Millie, Lillie was from a different world entirely (this one), and it was exactly what Walter needed.

They met at a farmers market, where Walter was admiring the various produce. Lillie was selling homemade jams and preserves at a nearby stall, and the two struck up a conversation. They talked about their mutual love for simple things and their appreciation for the beauty in life's small moments.

As Walter got to know Lillie, he found himself drawn to her kindness, her gentle spirit, and her unwavering devotion to living life on her own terms. She was a breath of fresh air, a reminder that there was more to life than just work and success.

Despite his reservations about getting involved with someone new, Walter couldn't resist the pull of Lillie's magnetic personality. They began dating, and as they spent more time together, Walter found himself feeling more alive and present than he had in years.

With Lillie by his side, Walter finally found the personal fulfillment he had been seeking for so long. They spent their days exploring the countryside, going on long walks, and simply enjoying each other's company.

For the first time in a long time, Walter felt truly happy. And he knew that with Lillie by his side, he had everything he needed to live a life filled with love, simplicity, and joy.

A Summer Fling To The X-Treme

A Summer Fling To The X-Treme

Chapter 21

Simpleville Forever

Millie stood on the outskirts of Simpleville, basking in the warm glow of the setting sun. Her heart felt lighter, filled with newfound appreciation for her hometown. She had traveled far and wide, searching for something elusive, only to realize that what she truly desired had been here all along.

Simpleville, with its familiar streets and tight-knit community, held a magic of its own. It was a place of genuine connections and a slower, more meaningful way of life. Millie regretted taking it for granted, now recognizing the true value of her roots.

Her thoughts turned to Samson, her loyal friend who had been there throughout her life. She had failed to see the affection and companionship that had blossomed between them, hidden beneath the guise of friendship. The realization hit her with force, and she couldn't ignore the depth of her feelings for him.

Tears welled up in Millie's eyes as she acknowledged her oversight. Samson had held her heart all along, his unwavering support and gentle kindness always by her side. Simpleville had become a mirror, reflecting the depth of their connection.

Determined to make things right, Millie ventured back into town. With each step, fueled by a renewed sense of purpose, she yearned to express her true feelings to Samson. Simpleville would become the backdrop for their love story, a place where their bond would evolve into something profound.

As she rode through the familiar streets, Millie's heart beat with anticipation. She was ready to tell Samson that he had always been more than a friend, and that she was ready to embark on a new chapter of their lives together. Her journey had led her to the person who had patiently waited for her to see what had been right in front of her all along.

Millie's heart raced as she rode up to Samson's fruit farm. The farm was as she remembered it, with rows of apple and peach trees stretching out to the horizon. Samson was working in the orchard, tending to the trees and humming a tune that she couldn't quite make out.

As she dismounted her horse, Millie took a moment to compose herself. She had rehearsed what she wanted to say to Samson, but now that the moment had arrived, her nerves were getting the better of her. She took a deep breath and stepped forward, her eyes fixed on Samson's broad shoulders.

"Samson," she called out, her voice barely above a whisper.

Samson turned around, his eyes widening in surprise as he caught sight of Millie. He wiped the sweat from his forehead and walked toward her, his expression a mix of confusion and joy.

"Millie," he said, his voice filled with disbelief. "You're back?!"

Millie took a step closer, her heart pounding in her chest. She looked up at Samson and saw the same warmth and kindness in his eyes that had always been there. She knew at that moment that she had made the right decision.

Millie took a deep breath, steadying her racing heart, and stepped closer to Samson, feeling a mixture of excitement and nervousness.

"Samson," she said, her voice filled with emotion. "I'm back. Forever."

A wide smile spread across Samson's face, mirroring the joy that swelled within him. He reached out and gently placed his hands on Millie's shoulders.

"Millie, I can't believe you're really here," he said, his voice filled with genuine happiness. "Tell me, how was your journey? Did you find what you were looking for out there?"

Millie's eyes sparkled as she began to recount her adventures, her voice laced with enthusiasm.

"Samson, it was incredible," she exclaimed. "I traveled across the country, met fascinating people, witnessed breathtaking landscapes, and experienced things I never thought possible."

Samson's curiosity was piqued as he listened intently to Millie's words.

Millie paused for a moment, "But why don't we go inside and talk about everything?" she said with a hint of hesitation in her voice.

As they sat inside, Millie's heart swelled with bittersweet memories as she sat across from Samson, recounting her time with Walter and the lessons she had learned. The warmth of the fire crackled in the cozy farmhouse, casting a gentle glow on their faces as Millie began to share her tale.

"Samson," she started, her voice tinged with nostalgia. "During my journey, I discovered that Walter was indeed a man of immense passion and purpose."

Millie took a deep breath, her eyes meeting Samson's with a mixture of anticipation and apprehension. Finally, she mustered the courage to reveal the truth.

"Samson," she said softly, "there's something I need to tell you about Walter. He wasn't from our time. He came from the future, on a mission to preserve the legacy of Smoothie King."

Samson's eyes widened in surprise as Millie's words hung in the air. His brows furrowed, trying to process the revelation. A mix of confusion, disbelief, and curiosity washed over his face, as he struggled to comprehend the enormity of what Millie had just shared. He took a moment, his mind racing with questions, before finally finding his voice.

"The future?" he exclaimed, his voice tinged with awe. "Walter came from the future? That's ... that's incredible! What ... What is Smoothie King?"

Samson's eyes sparkled with a newfound curiosity, eager to delve deeper into this extraordinary revelation and uncover the secrets that lay within the fabric of time.

Millie took a deep breath, realizing she needed to share another astonishing piece of information with Samson. She looked at him, her eyes filled with a mix of excitement and astonishment.

"Smoothie King is a renowned company known for its delicious and nutritious smoothies in the future. And it was actually started by your great great grandson."

Samson's eyes widened in disbelief, a hint of pride shining through. He leaned in, eager to hear more about this unexpected connection to a successful enterprise.

"He was inspired by the legacy of your fruit farm and the smoothies your family will pass down for generations," Millie continued. "Driven by a desire to bring health and happiness to people's lives, he built Smoothie King into a global brand that will touch the lives of countless individuals."

Samson's chest swelled with a mixture of astonishment and pride. The realization that his family's passion for fruit and smoothies had continued to thrive and evolve, transcending generations, brought a sense of joy and fulfillment.

"That's ... truly remarkable," Samson said, his voice filled with a mixture of awe and gratitude. "To think that something I started here with Walter has grown into such a meaningful legacy, benefiting people's well-being ... It's beyond anything I could have ever imagined. That's why he came here, isn't it?"

Millie nodded, her eyes shining with admiration. "It's a testament to the impact you have had, Samson. Your dedication to quality and your love for clean ingredients laid the foundation for a future that has touched lives far and wide."

Samson's heart swelled with pride and a renewed sense of purpose. He looked at Millie, a smile spreading across his face, as he realized the significance of his family's journey and the role they played in shaping a future where Smoothie King thrived.

"But where do the watermelons come in?" Samson asked, still confused.

Millie realized she had one more crucial piece of information to share with Samson. She looked at him, her eyes filled with a mix of urgency and determination.

"Samson, there's something else you need to know about Walter," she began. "He is not only from the future, but he is also the inventor of The X-Treme Watermelon Smoothie from Smoothie King, and he was on a mission to save the world."

Samson's eyes widened, captivated by the gravity of Millie's words. He leaned in closer, eager to hear the details of this extraordinary mission.

"In the future, summers have become unbearably hot," Millie continued. "People struggle to stay hydrated, and it has become a widespread problem. But Walter's invention, The X-Treme Watermelon Smoothie, has been a lifeline for countless individuals. It provides the necessary hydration and nourishment to endure the scorching heat."

Samson's heart raced as he realized the significance of Walter's invention. The thought that his great great grandson had played a crucial role in alleviating the suffering caused by extreme summers filled him with a profound sense of pride.

"But there's a problem," Millie continued, her voice tinged with concern. "The watermelon seeds in the future are on the brink of extinction. Without them, the production of The X-Treme Watermelon Smoothie is at risk. That's why Walter traveled back in time, to collect as many watermelon seeds as he could and bring them back to the future, to save the world."

Samson's eyes widened in astonishment and concern. The weight of the mission, the urgency to preserve the watermelon seeds and ensure the future's survival, settled upon him like a heavy burden.

"It's a lot to take in." Millie said, looking at Samson with all of the compassion in the world. "I, too, had to process this information.

Samson then wondered what this meant for Millie and Walter. "Is Walter going to come back to be with you?"

Samson asked, not knowing if he wanted to know the answer.

Millie looked at Samson, realizing that this was the moment she could reveal to him all of her true feelings.

"No, he isn't," Millie responded with a slight smile.

"Walter knew the consequences of his actions, the ripple effects they would have on the lives of many," Millie continued. "Walter understood the importance of sacrifice, of putting the needs of others before his own desires. He had a deep sense of responsibility, a commitment to a greater purpose."

Millie paused for a moment, her gaze meeting Samson's. "And that's why he had to make the difficult decision to return to his time, to fulfill his mission. As much as it pained both of us, we knew that the future needed him, needed his knowledge and expertise. The impact of Smoothie King on people's lives, the happiness and nourishment it brought—it was something worth fighting for."

A mix of emotions flickered across Millie's face as she concluded her account. "I learned that love isn't always about holding on; sometimes, it's about letting go for the greater good. Walter's love for what he did, his love for the people who would be affected by his actions, guided his choices. It was a love that transcended time and space, and it's something I will always carry with me."

Millie's voice trailed off, the weight of her experiences with Walter lingering in the air. She and Samson sat in silence for a moment, reflecting on the journey that had brought them together and the lessons they had learned from it. The fire crackled, casting dancing shadows on the walls, as Millie's heart brimmed with gratitude for the time she had spent with Walter and the impact he had made on her life.

Millie took a deep breath, as she looked into Samson's eyes, her voice trembling with vulnerability yet filled with sincerity.

"Samson, there's one more thing I need to tell you," she began, her voice laced with emotion. "I could have gone back to the future with Walter, to be by his side. The idea of a life filled with uncertainty and unknowns was both exhilarating and terrifying."

Samson listened intently, his gaze locked with Millie's, sensing the weight of her words.

"But during my journey, I had a profound experience," Millie continued. "I visited a psychic who had a crystal ball. As she gazed into it, she saw my true desire, my deepest longing. And in that crystal ball, Samson, she saw you."

A flicker of surprise and curiosity danced across Samson's face, his attention fully captured by Millie's revelation.

"She saw moments we had shared, laughter, and warmth," Millie's voice quivered with emotion. "She saw my future with you, Samson. A future filled with love, companionship, and a deep connection. At the moment I tried to brush off what I saw as friendship, but now I know where my heart truly belongs."

Samson's eyes widened, a mix of surprise and joy lighting up his face. He reached out, gently taking Millie's hand in his, feeling a surge of emotion coursing through him.

"I've known you my whole life, Samson," Millie continued, her voice filled with sincerity, "and over the years, you've shown me kindness, understanding, and a love for life that resonates with my own. Being with you feels like coming home, like finding a missing piece of my heart."

Samson's heart swelled with emotion, his grip on Millie's hand tightening as he absorbed her words. The revelation of her feelings left him both elated and humbled.

"I made the choice to come back, Samson, because my heart told me that the future I truly desired was right here, with you," Millie said, her voice filled with conviction. "Being with you, working together to preserve the legacy of smoothies, and sharing a life filled with love and purpose—that's where I find my happiness."

A tear glistened in Samson's eye as he nodded, his voice filled with tenderness. "Millie, you've touched my heart in ways I can't put into words. To know that you see a future with me, that our paths have finally aligned, fills me with an indescribable joy. I've always been in love with you, Millie, deeply and completely."

Millie's face lit up with a radiant smile, her heart brimming with love and hope. She knew that she had made the right choice, that destiny had brought them together for a reason.

As they stood there, hand in hand, their hearts intertwined, Millie and Samson felt a profound sense of gratitude for the journey that had led them to this moment.

A Summer Fling To The X-Treme

Chapter 22
The Last Sip

Millie and Samson had found their bliss in the simplicity of life together. Their days were filled with laughter, love, and the beautiful chaos that came with raising three adventurous children. But amidst the joy, there lingered a familiar longing, a shared understanding that their children desired more than what Simpleville could offer.

Their wild children, brimming with dreams and curiosity, yearned to explore the world beyond the familiar streets and quiet countryside. Millie and Samson empathized with their yearning, for they too had once felt the pull of the unknown. They knew all too well the desire to seek something beyond the boundaries of Simpleville.

As their children spread their wings, Millie and Samson found solace in knowing that their offspring had inherited the same spirit of adventure that had once burned within them. They encouraged their children to embrace the world with open hearts and reminded them that Simpleville would always be their anchor—a place they could return to, where the love of family would forever await them.

Meanwhile, the townspeople of Simpleville continued to marvel at the enigmatic figure of Walter Melone, who had mysteriously appeared and disappeared from their lives. Speculation swirled among them, and they constantly sought answers from Millie and Samson. But the couple, knowing the significance of Walter's mission, chose to keep his true fate a secret. Whenever questioned, they would simply reply, "Oh, he went away on business," leaving the townspeople to wonder about the truth that only they knew.

For Samson, now knowing about Smoothie King, it had forever changed his perspective. He could never bring himself to sell smoothies again, feeling a deeper calling within him. He understood that his purpose extended beyond the confines of Simpleville. Samson felt the weight of his family lineage, a responsibility to pass down his knowledge and the secrets of creating the ultimate meal in a cup—one that would revolutionize the way people nourished their bodies.

With unwavering dedication, Samson took on the role of guardian of the family legacy, patiently waiting for the world to be truly ready for the ultimate replacement. He immersed himself in research, exploring the realms of nutrition, clean ingredients, and whole fruits. Samson knew that his calling was not only to create a powerful and nutritious beverage but to ensure that it would be a gift bestowed upon the world at the perfect moment.

In the quiet moments shared between Millie and Samson, they reveled in the memories they had created together and the beautiful life they had built in Simpleville. They found contentment in the simplicity of their days, surrounded by the love of their growing family and the close-knit community they cherished.

Simpleville remained a place of comfort and nostalgia, where the townspeople continued to share stories of Walter Melone, forever intrigued by the mysterious traveler who had left an indelible mark on their small town. And as Millie and Samson watched their children set off on their own grand adventures, they smiled, knowing that the spirit of wanderlust and the legacy of Walter's journey would forever be woven into the fabric of their lives.

In this chapter of their story, Millie and Samson found fulfillment in the simple joys of love, family, and community. They embraced their roles as guardians of both their family's legacy and the secrets yet to be revealed. And in their hearts, they held the unwavering hope that one day, the world would be ready to taste the power-packed, nutritionally rich cup that Samson had so passionately crafted—a testament to their commitment to a healthier, more vibrant future.

Made in United States
Orlando, FL
27 May 2023

33547812R00139